FINDING ECSTASY 10TH ANNIVERSARY EDITION

NORMAN FOX

AUTHOR'S NOTE

This story is based on my personal experiences over a nine-year period. The names and the identifying characteristics of the persons who appear in this story have been altered and some characters have been combined. Certain events and situations have also been imaginatively transformed, and those events and situations are not intended to portray actual events and situations.

Please be aware that this story contains content that may be distressing and triggering for some people. If you need assistance or support, please contact one of the following organisations:

Beyond Blue
1300 22 4636
beyondflue.org.au
or
Lifeline
13 11 14
lifeline.org.au

DEDICATION

This book is dedicated to my amazing, talented, and loving husband, Stephen Sander, my supportive parents, Roslyn and Harold Fox, and to *The Group* (you know who you are).

FOREWORD

FINDING ECSTASY IS now 10 years old. It was written as a cautionary tale for teenagers and parents, and as a trip down memory lane for people who love a good party with electronic dance music and illegal stimulants.

Many of the controversial issues and situations described in Finding Ecstasy, including bullying, homophobia, underage drug usage, and underage sex, have not changed substantially in the 40 years since the story took place in the mid to late 1980s.

The events that lead an underage boy named Nathan to seek out affection from older men because he couldn't dare be openly gay in the school playground, is still a struggle that many LGBTQ+ youth face. However, this situation appears to be changing. For example, at more progressive schools, same-sex couples have been proudly bringing their same-sex partners to high school events, a positive sign that teen attitudes towards same-sex couples is progressing, which is wonderful.

However, there are still schools where bringing your same-sex partner to a school event is strictly forbidden. Being in the closet because others insist that a member of the LGBTQ+ repress who they are, is unhealthy. Research has shown it can contribute to negative psychological conditions and, sadly, self-harm.

Nor have we evolved very far as a society when it comes to the so-called War on Drugs. Mere harm reduction strategies are still debated by governments. Some cities in Australia, such as Canberra, have done pill testing trials with positive results. However, in general, pill testing is still a divisive topic and has yet to be implemented for the tens of thousands of people who attend raves and music festivals. Pill testing is a subject that even politicians struggle to talk about, let alone implement for the safety of party goers. This is despite multiple drug-related hospitalisations and deaths at raves and music festivals each year. *Finding Ecstasy's* main character, Nathan, and his friends in The Group, would have benefitted from pill testing had it existed at the time. According to the 2019 National Drug Strategy Household Survey (NDSHS), an estimated 9 million people aged 14 and over in Australia (43% of the population) had illicitly used a drug at some point in their lifetime. I was one of them and *Finding Ecstasy* is my story of how and why it can so easily happen to any teenager. The 2019 the Australian Election Study survey found 63% of Australians supported pill testing, with only 21% directly opposed.

When it comes to bullying and homophobia, we still have a long way to go, both locally and globally. In Australia, research substantiates that sexual and/or gender minority students are disproportionately affected by bullying relative to their heterosexual peers. Is it any wonder that many younger members of the LGBTQ+ community still choose to stay in the closet or turn to drugs?

This is a story of my childhood and how I did not cope with my own sexual orientation from a young age. I hope you find it enlightening. Being bullied by other students for being gay can lead to negative outcomes and I found acceptance through the dance party scene, even if it did leave me with some psychological scars in the process.

If you're an adult in the electronic dance music scene, enjoy and play safe.

PROLOGUE

1989

After we tried ecstasy, everyone at school called us The Group.

SCORING

FEBRUARY 1989, SYDNEY, AUSTRALIA

AT SIXTEEN YEARS old, I had my parents so well trained that they hid in their bedroom whenever my friends rang the doorbell on a Saturday night. Like any normal teenager, I made it clear to Mum and Dad that they were a complete embarrassment, and I was utterly ashamed of them. But I liked how they let me take over their living room for my friends to hang out in, before we headed off to another dance party.

When I opened the front door, despite having warned them away earlier, Mum tried to greet my friends. I practically exploded. "I told you, they're here to see me — not you!"

"Okay! Okay, I'm going!" Mum disappeared up the stairs.

"I can't believe how you treat your parents!" Evelyn grinned when I let her in.

"Yeah, mine would kill me if I acted like that!" said Anna.

"Mine are used to it." I grinned back mischievously.

By 9 p.m., the whole group had arrived.

We took photos of each other proudly holding our Fun Love Hordern Pavilion dance party tickets and wearing our new going-out uniforms: 501 Levi Jeans, Doc Martin shoes, smiley-face t-shirts, waistcoats, and bandanas.

"Pose-mode!" We cheered as the flash bulb went off.

Each shot captured our over-excited mood. I posed with my crew from Dover Heights High: Anna, Evelyn, Lee, Sarah, and Simon. We acted like models in front of the camera. I couldn't wait to get the photos developed on Monday afternoon. All the other kids at school would be so jealous.

By 10 p.m., we left my place and caught the 380 bus to Oxford Street and got off at Paddington Town Hall, then walked down to the Royal Sydney Showground. In the night air, a deep bass beat belted through the darkness. Outside the gates of the Hordern Pavilion, masses of party people were already queuing to get in.

We joined them and handed our tickets to the security staff at the turnstiles, praying they wouldn't ask for an ID. The Fun Love party was for over 18s. Luckily, no one questioned our real age as we did our best to blend in with the cool party people.

At the turnstile, we were handed mini show-bags, which contained a masquerade mask, glow stick, whistle, and a tiny bubble blower kit. Beyond the gates, we could see a familiar sight of carnival rides — dodgem car stand, mini-Ferris wheel, and bouncy castle — it was all kids' stuff.

But this was no kids' party.

We were on a mission.

"Got to find a dealer!"

We scoped the masses for that special someone.

What I'd said made Evelyn look instantly uncomfortable. She couldn't believe the rest of us had decided to try ecstasy. Evelyn didn't believe in doing drugs. She was the only one there just to dance. The rest of us had been there and done that, and now were ready for more.

I remembered how, when I was younger, I also used to fear drugs. But since I'd discovered the world of dance parties at the Hordern, that had all changed. Now I was on the hunt to find a dealer to sell us what we wanted: ecstasy. Tonight was serious business. We had to find someone who wouldn't try to take advantage of us. We were first timers. We had to find someone who wouldn't try to rip us off or sell us duds, or worse, someone who was an undercover police officer from the drug squad.

Then we'd be in deep shit!

"So, what does an ecstasy dealer look like?" Anna asked as we scanned the crowd.

The very thought of what we were doing filled us with excitement.

It was fun and kind of scary, not to mention illegal.

Out of all the kids at school, our gang was the most unlikely to be thought of as drug users. We were in the A-Grade. We got the best marks and never got detention for misbehaving. The rougher kids at school called us nerds.

The popular, surfy kids at school didn't think much of us. I think they hated us because we were so different from everyone else. We stood out. At Dover, most kids hung out with their own clan. If you were Anglo, Asian, Jewish, or an Islander, you hung out with your own kind. But with my friends, we had one of each.

Evelyn had chocolate brown skin and exotic Tongan features. She was one of the most beautiful girls at school and one of the shyest. Only when she was with us, and on the dance floor, was she comfortable enough to let herself loosen up.

Anna was Jewish and originally from Austria. She had long blond hair and had come to Australia when she was nine years old. She lived just with her mum, who had recently converted to Krishna Consciousness. They were sort of in-between religions.

Lee and Simon were my best mates and were both Asian. Lee had thick black, spiky hair. He'd come to Australia from China when he was five years old but now said, *"mate"* with a thicker Aussie accent than I did.

Simon was from Vietnam. His family had migrated to Australia in the 70s in a boat following the war. Now his father owned a successful take-away food store in China Town.

Sarah was from South America and was the toughest of our group. She'd gotten detention once for punching another girl who'd called her a wog in year 7. Sarah had a mop of fiery red hair and bright blue eyes and didn't care who she pissed off at school.

I was the only Anglo Aussie kid in my gang. I was also the only one who got teased for being a fag, something I strenuously insisted I wasn't. I ignored the taunts of the alpha males in the school playground who called me names for a sport.

The other kids at school didn't know how to take us. We didn't fit in with the formula of the other groups in the playground. They all gossiped about who was going out with whom within our group. They had done the math. Three boys plus three girls equaled that we were *going around with each other*. And *going around with each other* meant you were boyfriend and girlfriend. We weren't; we just didn't like any of the other dickheads from school.

"We must be the biggest dorks ever if we can't score E at a party like this," Sarah said as we scoped the crowd gathering outside the Hordern. Thousands of people were set to have the best night of their lives and we were dying to be a part of it. At least one of them had to be selling drugs. Why else would so many of these party people be grinning from ear to ear?

"You guys are idiots if you go through with this!" warned Evelyn, shaking her head disapprovingly as we found ourselves giving random party people a rating out of ten for their likeliness to be a drug dealer.

"Five," Lee said pointing at a man who was grinning with wide eyes and bouncing up and down.

"Yeah, he looks like he's on something," Sarah agreed.

In that instant, we all simultaneously spotted another man in the crowd and had the same gut reaction — we'd found who would hopefully be our trusty drug dealer.

"Ten!"

All of us burst into laughter, except for Evelyn.

This guy looked much older than most people at the party. He had long, sandy blond hair tied in a ponytail and wore a white singlet with black bicycle shorts, dirty Dunlop volley shoes, and had a black leather bum-bag around his waist. He seemed to be scoping the crowd just like we were. But what made him stand out most was the way he couldn't stand still. He was almost dancing on the spot as he worked his way through the crowd. Some party people greeted him with open arms and others shook their heads as if saying no, after which he'd move on to the next gang of party people.

"You can't be serious." Evelyn's jaw dropped.

"He looks pretty dodgy!" Lee sided with Evelyn.

"I bet he knows where we could get some," Sarah said.

"Whoever he is, he's definitely on something," I responded.

"Well, let's not just stand here all night watching him. It's freaky." Evelyn rolled her eyes. "Are we going to hit the dance floor or what?"

I kept my eyes on our suspected drug dealer as he also entered the Hordern Pavilion. Inside, the dance floor was bursting with over a thousand people moving to the pumping house beat. There was cheering, smiling, and arms stretched towards the pulsating laser lights shining through the darkness.

We felt so cool being a part of this event, way cooler than any of the other kids from school. Just being on the dance floor felt like we were part of something bigger and more incredible than our 'secret lives' of being mere high school students from Dover Heights High.

The DJ was elevated above the floor on a stage that overlooked an expansive dance space. Suspended above the crowd were giant fluorescent polystyrene love hearts, smiley faces, and massive capsule-shaped pills next to enormous twirling mirror balls.

Inner City's song, *Big Fun,* boomed from the massive speakers, as our eyes remained glued to who we hoped would soon become our first drug dealer.

Each of us did our best to dance cool and fit in with the gathering crowd, trying to act like we belonged. I watched with anticipation as a young guy and girl approached our suspected dealer. The guy gave him money and the dealer looked around cautiously before reaching into his bum bag and handing something back. The guy and girl suddenly looked thrilled before they disappeared off the dance floor.

The dealer stayed on the floor and continued to check out the growing crowd of smiling, dancing party people.

"That confirms it!" Anna yelled over the music.

"This is our chance." Sarah tugged at my arm.

"Go on Nathan, you ask him!" Lee urged.

I was being peer pressured into scoring drugs for my friends by my friends. How could I say no? With my heart racing, I approached the dealer with Simon by my side for support.

I was frightened the dealer would reject me, just as others had done at the previous Black Party. This was our second dance party since the New Year's Eve RAT Party and so far, we'd been completely unsuccessful in our search for ecstasy.

As I approached the dealer, I could smell an acidic odor that was overwhelming.

"Got any eckie?" I tried to sound like I knew what I was talking about.

"$20 each," he said without missing a beat, but sounded stand-offish. Up close, his face was extremely wrinkled. He was probably in his late 40s and his pupils were giant black holes, bulging unnaturally large and reflecting the flashing-coloured lights shining above us.

"Can I have five?"

"$100."

No one else could hear us against the thunderous acid house music the DJ blasted, Yazz's *The only way is up*.

I handed the dealer one-hundred-dollars of my friends' pocket money, and he placed five pills in my palm.

"They're called green meanies," he said.

I smiled and held onto the pills tightly.

"I'm Steven. I'm at most parties, if you ever need something."

"Thanks!" I couldn't believe it was that easy. We had found our ecstasy!

Simon and I returned to our friends, who'd been watching us score with much excitement. Anna, Lee, and Sarah looked like they were going to burst, while Evelyn danced alongside them with an expression of disapproval.

"Let's go somewhere private," I said.

It wasn't very easy to do this at a dance party with several thousand people. We bought a bottle of water and headed for the stadium seating at the back of the Pavilion. High above the dance floor, I opened the palm of my hand and flashed our purchase. There I was, holding five chunky white pills with green speckles.

"What if they're not real?" Evelyn shrugged concerned.

None of us answered Evelyn. Our minds had been made up. We ignored thoughts about all those stories about how dealers cut their drugs with Ajax cleaning power.

I licked one of the pills as my friends looked at theirs.

Lee and Simon did the same and licked their pills. It was like we hoped that by tasting them it would somehow confirm that they contained the real thing. But when our tongues tasted the substance our faces twisted in disgust, reacting to its acidic, unnatural taste.

"Yuck. It tastes filthy!" Lee spat.

"At least we didn't pay $20 each for a headache pill," Simon reasoned.

As I took mine, I looked into my friends' eyes — feeling fear and excitement in equal doses.

Hoping for the best, we each took a massive chance and swallowed the chunky pills with a sip of mineral water while Evelyn watched on, still disapproving.

"No way. You guys are crazy!"

SMOKING

1981, EASTERN SUBURBS

MY VERY FIRST experience with drugs had been when I'd learnt how to smoke at nine-years-old. I was in the out-of-bounds zone, hidden away from view of the teachers, behind the girls' toilet block. I was with Tiffany, a girl who lived on the same street as me. Tiffany and I had been friends since we were six years old.

"I stole them from my Mum's handbag," Tiffany said as she pulled a box of Benson & Hedges Extra Mild from her backpack. She struck the match that got me started.

The label, WARNING SMOKING IS A HEALTH HAZARD, was hardly a deterrent, and not just because I was slightly dyslexic and a slow learner. On my first go, I eagerly sucked the cigarette, wanting to see what all the fuss was about. But nothing happened. Instead of puffing smoke, I made the filter go soggy.

"You do it like this." Tiffany rolled her eyes as she demonstrated and took another drag.

The tobacco turned red and cigarette smoke swirled between us.

"How do you do that?" I asked.

"You have to draw it in," Tiffany explained, wise beyond her years. Tiffany was proof that girls mature faster than boys.

I took another drag and this time it tasted disgusting. But I didn't care because I was so proud of myself after I left faint traces of smoke in the air.

"Tastes good, hey?" Tiffany smiled.

"Sure does!" I began to cough uncontrollably. My eyes filled with tears, and I had to spit out the awful taste. My saliva landed on the gravel near Tiffany's shiny black school shoes.

"God, Nathan, you're so gross!" She frowned.

"Have you been smoking?" My mum knew exactly what I'd been up to the minute I got home. She smelt my fingers and my school uniform, and her voice went up an octave, "How could you do something so stupid?"

"I didn't do it. I… I…was just holding it for a friend."

"Rubbish! You're never to smoke again, Nathan! Do you understand me?"

Mum dobbed on me to Dad.

"You bloody idiot!" He fumed when he came home from work. Dad went on and on about how I was too young to smoke and how smoking was bad for my health. He banned me from playing Atari for a whole week as punishment.

It was so unfair!

Both my parents were non-smokers. They had no idea what it was like.

1984

"You're going to have to act normal next year," my best friend Michael told me after we found out which high schools we were going to.

"What do you mean?" I asked.

"Well, here, we know what you're like. We're used to you being…a total attention seeker! But at Dover, they're going to think you're a real weirdo!"

"Will not!" I protested.

Michael gave me a look that said, *'Yes they will!'*

So, I did a loud, stinky burp in his face to prove what a weirdo really was.

"How dare you!" Michael put on a posh English accent, pretending to sound like his mother. His voice didn't match the slightly overweight boy standing in front of me with his rosy cheeks and shiny blond hair. Michael's impression of his mum cracked us both up. For twelve-year-old boys, we were both weirdos.

In grade four, my teacher Mrs Lewis put Michael and I into separate classes because she couldn't control us. She accused me of being the class clown. In my report card, Mrs Lewis wrote:

"Nathan is a bright student. He is creative and artistic. However, he is easily led and tends to interrupt the class and distract fellow students. If Nathan does not change his behavior, he will disadvantage himself and will not achieve his full potential."

Mum fretted upon reading Mrs Lewis' report. "What are we going to do with you?" She sighed.

I was sitting in front of the TV playing Space Invaders on the Atari.

"You better start behaving yourself," Mum warned as I scored 100 points for shooting down the *mother ship.*

"Yes!" I cheered at the TV, completely ignoring my mum.

Mum turned to Dad in frustration. He was reading The Sydney Morning Herald. "Have you read this?" She shoved my report card in Dad's face.

Both my parents were working class. Dad worked for Australia Post and Mum worked for a clothing manufacturer. I don't think either of them liked their jobs, but they had to work hard because, as my Mum constantly reminded me, "We never got any hand-outs from our parents!"

Money was tight. Yet, we lived in a nice big home in the Eastern suburbs near Centennial Park. However, that didn't make home a happy place. The one thing I hated most about my parents was that they'd fight over the littlest things, like breaking a dish when doing the washing up or when Dad lost his wallet somewhere in Bondi Junction. When they fought, I'd turn up the sound on the TV or the stereo. Sometimes I had to yell at my parents, telling them to stop fighting, "Shut up!" That's when they'd tell me to go to my room and not to speak to them like that. I learned early that being disrespectful to my parents worked to quieten them down.

The truth is that both my Mum and Dad were very kind. I knew they wanted the best for me and occasionally told me that I was spoiled. I was an only child and when I was good around the house, Mum would take me to the record shop, my favorite place in the world. Mum would buy me the latest LP I wanted.

By the time I hit puberty, I had a sizeable collection of pop albums and 12-inch remixes, like *Material Girl* by Madonna, *Girls just wanna have fun* by Cyndi Lauper, and *Sweet Dreams* by Eurythmics. At the time, neither me, nor my parents, appreciated how camp my taste was in music.

It turned out Mrs Lewis was right. I did disadvantage myself. I didn't get pre-selected to attend the high school of my dreams. I wanted to go to Sydney Boys High, a selective school, and the best in the neighborhood. But for me it was game over. My test score didn't pass the necessary grade and I was enrolled to attend Dover Heights High School instead, a co-educational public school that had the worst reputation in the Eastern suburbs!

No one wanted to go there. It didn't matter that Dover was in one of the most prestigious postcodes of Sydney, or that the views from the school playground included the Sydney Opera House and the Harbour Bridge. While Dover had 'location, location, location,' it was also the school where all the dregs ended up. Everyone knew you only went to Dover if your parents couldn't afford to send you to a private school or, if you were like me or Tiffany, not smart enough to get into a selective school.

"Know what I heard about Dover?" Tiffany asked as we walked home from school.

"What?"

"Cheryl said she heard a girl at Dover was pushed into taking drugs!"

"Really?"

"Mmm-hmm. The senior girls grabbed her in the toilets and forced her to buy drugs off them. Or else."

"Or else what?"

"They would flush her head down the dunny can!"

I pictured Tiffany's head being forced into a toilet bowl by older girls as they reached for the chain to flush, and the prospect of going to Dover just got worse. "We have to look out for each other next year when we start high school!"

Tiffany opened her backpack to offer me a cigarette.

I lit up and took a drag without coughing. Now that I was twelve years old and more experienced, I knew how important it was to blow the smoke away from my uniform. That way, Mum couldn't smell it on me when I got home. Also, chewing gum cleaned the breath.

Tiffany was tough and a bit of a tomboy. She had no fear, not only did she teach me how to smoke, but she also protected me from the bully who lived between us on our street, an older skater kid named Sean. He used to threaten to bash me up if I passed his house because he thought I was a poofter. Tiffany would walk with me past his place to make sure Sean didn't try anything. This was after he'd once chased me down the street ready to bash me up.

I think Tiffany liked me because I could always make her laugh. She made me feel funny and alive. I was the class clown, after all. Also, when we would soon hit our teenage years, I was the only boy Tiffany knew who didn't try to pressure her into having sex.

Even though I tried cigarettes early in life, before I started high school, the idea of illegal drugs scared me to death. All I knew about drugs was what I'd seen on TV.

One time, on the current affairs program Dad watched, Willesee interviewed a sixteen-year-old boy, Greg, a drug-addicted male prostitute who worked 'The Wall' at Darlinghurst near Kings Cross. At the time I had no idea what this really meant, but I knew it must be very bad if it was on TV. I played with my space Lego building blocks while my parents watched the interview from the sofa.

"How often do you take drugs?" Willesee asked.

"I'm stoned right now," Greg replied casually.

"You mean you are high right now?" Willesee asked just as casually.

"Yep," Greg shrugged.

"Poor kid," my Mum sighed.

I looked at Greg on the TV. He had dark hair like mine but looked rough, wearing a black leather jacket, and had tattoos on his neck. Greg admitted he didn't mind having sex with men for money when he was on heroin. *"I sort of enjoy it when I'm out-of-it."* He shrugged.

I hadn't even known men could have sex with one another! I listened closely, feeling curious and repulsed. I wondered what high school Greg went to. I hoped it wasn't Dover Heights.

"Why do you do it?" Willesee asked.

"Don't know…" Greg shrugged.

Mum told Dad I was too young to be watching this.

Dad switched the channel to Mum's favourite TV drama series, *Sons & Daughters*.

The only other impression I had about drugs growing up came from a TV commercial that interrupted the afternoon cartoons. It started off in black and white and showed a thin, older teenage girl sitting alone in a dark room. Her face looked so gross. It was diseased and had lots of scabs.

"There isn't much more drugs can take from me," she said as the commercial began to show photos of a teenage girl taken when she was younger, when she was around our age. She used to look so pretty. *"Drugs have stolen my friends."* The photos showed her smiling and hugging a group of girlfriends in school uniforms. She used to look like Tiffany. They had the same pretty yet tough tomboy looks, with short wispy black hair, a cute button nose and ruby red lips. *"Drugs have stolen my family and self-respect."* More photographs appeared, showing the girl on screen with her parents, then another in her bedroom holding a Siamese cat and, in the last photo, she was with an older boy wearing a black leather jacket. *"There isn't anything else heroin can take from me. Except maybe my life."*

As she said this, she stared straight out from the TV screen. It was a government TV advertisement and, when I was twelve years old, it did its job in convincing me never to try heroin.

On the last day of primary school, all the year 6 kids' school uniforms had farewell messages scribbled on them in permanent markers: *"Best friends forever"*, *"Stay in touch!"* and *"High school here we come!"*.

I was wondering what high school would be like as I shared my last cigarette behind the toilet block with Tiffany and Michael. "I'm never going to do drugs," I announced.

"But what if you are forced?" Tiffany raised her brow coolly.

I felt nauseous when she said this, and by the way she said this, like it was inevitable. My mouth even filled with saliva, and it wasn't just the cigarette that was making me feel sick. It was the thought of what we faced.

"Yeah, Nathan. What are you going to do if they try to force you to take drugs?" Michael grabbed the cigarette from my fingers and took a drag. "I've heard the kids at Dover are pretty rough."

"Well, I won't let them!" I spat to look tough and to get rid of the horrible nicotine taste from my mouth. I was jealous of Michael. He was enrolled to go to Sydney Boys High School. I believed he'd be safe there.

"Yeah, I don't believe in doing drugs!" Michael coughed up a nicotine-spit ball that matched mine.

"What about marijuana?" Tiffany asked.

"No way!" I shook my head. "On Willesee, I saw how this guy went from smoking one puff of marijuana to hard drugs like heroin, and you don't want to know what else he was doing! He reckoned once you try heroin that was it — you're addicted for life!"

BOOZE

1986, DOVER HEIGHTS HIGH SCHOOL

TIFFANY AND I were put into different classes at Dover Heights. I was in the A-Grade with the incredibly smart Asian and Jewish kids. Tiffany was in the D-Grade with the smart-ass Aussie surfy crowd. She soon became one of the most popular girls in school. Tiffany had the coolest haircut, a fringe that had been bleached blond, and she wore dark eyeliner. Plus, she was the first girl at school to buy a pair of Doc Martin shoes.

I had pimples, braces, hairy legs, and a girlie-sounding voice. I was one of the most picked on boys in the playground.

Going to Dover was a real adjustment. Unlike at Woollahra, I was no longer the popular class clown who kept all the kids entertained. At Dover, I was an easy target for the tough kids. It scared me just to be around them. Especially because the tough kids agreed that I was a fag, something I desperately spent my time trying to convince anyone who'd listen that I wasn't.

At Dover, I was sort of popular with the girls. I knew how to make them laugh and essentially liked the same things they did: Dynasty and Dolly Doctor. I liked the same TV shows and music. I thought the boys at high school didn't like me because I was getting along with the girls, while they were the ones who didn't know how to talk to them. I suspected that they were probably just jealous of me. What choice did they have but to label me a fag? It was something that I explained away to the girls by saying the Dover boys were a bunch of jealous losers.

At Dover Heights High, we were taught that nicotine was a drug and that smoking was addictive. But by the time the teachers held a drug education discussion in year 8, I had been smoking for four years and some of the other kids had already begun to educate themselves about marijuana. We were so far ahead of the teachers that we could have educated them on drugs.

It wasn't like anyone got forced into taking drugs in the school toilets like Tiffany and I had been scared into believing. Instead, it all happened outside of school. Like when word got around that Tiffany was having a party at her place on Friday night while her Mum was away. All the cool kids planned to be there. Tiffany forced me to come along in the hope that they'd get to like me.

I felt like I was risking my life by going to Tiffany's party. I went along because what I really wanted, more than anything, was to be popular. Even just being liked would be a start. Then, hopefully, they'd stop calling me a faggot, or so I thought.

That night, Tiffany's apartment was full of cigarette smoke and D-Graders dancing to Midnight Oil. Their heads bounced to thrashing rock guitar and Peter Garret screeching from the speakers, *"We've got the best of both worlds!"*

The music put me on edge. It sounded like it had been made by a group of escaped mental patients and it was making the D-Graders dance like crazy. I didn't really get into Aussie rock bands. There was no INXS or Midnight Oil in my record collection.

"Hey, Tiff!" Matt yelled. He was a fifteen-year-old surfy grommet dressed in loose fitting Billabong board shorts. "Know what KB stands for?" He was holding a can of KB Lager.

"What?" the D-Graders cheered.

"Kids Beer!" Matt burped and they all burst into laughter.

Tiffany looked at me like I should be laughing too.

"Good one, Matt!" I said, feeling tense as I sipped lemonade from a can.

"Shut-up, fag!" Matt sneered before he grabbed Tiffany's arm, dragging her towards the bedroom and spilling his kids beer all over the carpet.

The only people from the A-Grade at Tiffany's party that I knew were Evelyn and Anna. I was surprised to see them there because Tiffany never talked to them at school. Anna and Evelyn were good girls. They sat at the front of the class, did their homework, and never misbehaved.

Anna was one of the prettiest girls in the room. Her long blond hair was tied into pigtails, she had pale skin, blue-eyes, and wore a neat, white cotton dress. None of the D-Graders talked to her. Unlike some of the girls in Tiffany's class, Anna hadn't started wearing makeup or lost her virginity.

Evelyn looked more adult and dressed funky, wearing a Bob Marley singlet, miniskirt, and large gold-hoop earrings. It was a different side to the girl I knew from school, who was usually very quiet and avoided attention.

"What are you guys doing here?" I asked them.

"We got invited by Evelyn's older brother." Anna nodded towards Shane.

Shane was in year 10, the tallest boy in the room, and was carrying a Bottle Shop bag filled with booze. The D-Graders began to chant Shane's name as they surrounded him to get more kids beer.

"I wish we didn't come." Anna sighed.

"Shoosh!" Evelyn looked horrified. "Someone might hear you!"

"So what?" Anna folded her arms. "They're too drunk to care. They're acting like a bunch of dickheads!"

"Tiffany's mum is going to kill her when she sees this place," I agreed.

"Seriously, guys, loosen up. It's the 80s!" Evelyn flicked her thick, long black hair to act all sophisticated and grown-up.

Without saying a word to Anna or Evelyn, Tiffany grabbed my hand and giggled in my ear, "Time to get tipsy!" In her other hand was a six-pack of West Coast Cooler.

As Tiffany led me towards the bathroom, I heard Evelyn say something that really hurt, "What's the most popular girl in school doing hanging with such a geek?"

The *dickheads* begun chanting, "Scull! Scull! Scull!" to Shane and Matt, who were holding a drinking competition.

Tiffany locked the bathroom door and opened two bottles of West Coast Cooler. "Cheers!" She slammed her bottle against mine then swallowed the wine cooler in a single go. Unlike me, it was not the first time Tiffany had tried alcohol. She'd started drinking in year 7, not long after she'd started at Dover. She'd also lost her virginity that same year. She bragged about it, like it wasn't a big deal. When Tiffany finished her first bottle, she burped out loud like a boy.

I smirked and took a sip. I couldn't taste the alcohol. West Coast Cooler was fruity, like lemonade mixed with cordial, and sickly sweet.

Tiffany jumped into the bathtub and started to dance, pretending the empty West Coast Cooler bottle was a microphone, belting out her own slurred version of Cyndi Lauper's, *'Girls just wanna to have fun'*. With pink lipstick, smudged eyeliner, and teased hair, Tiffany looked older than the average fourteen-year-old girl.

I took a bigger gulp from my West Coast Cooler to catch up with her and felt more at ease. All week, I'd been so nervous about coming to Tiffany's party. I thought the D-Graders would give me such a hard time for turning up. As it turned out, drinking wine cooler in the bathtub with my best friend beat my usual Friday night.

Normally, when I got home on a Friday afternoon, I tore off my uniform and checked out my face in the mirror. *So ugly*, I thought as my reflection stared back at me. I had shiny metal braces and pimples, which I spent half an hour popping, squirting puss onto my reflection. After I popped every white head I could see, I applied Clearasil cream, which stung like hell.

That's how my week normally ended since hitting puberty and

starting at Dover Heights High. Popping pimples is how I forgot about being called faggot all week by the kids at school. Those words stung more than the Clearasil did on my popped pimples. When Michael had said the kids at Dover would call me a weirdo, he was wrong. They yelled at me names like poofter, fairy, and faggot. By the end of each week, I'd be so agitated I wouldn't want to talk to anyone. Not even my mum.

The factory Mum worked for in the city made football jerseys for the National Rugby League, which meant I had an endless supply of free rugby jerseys of every team. This was so ironic because I hated sports. I couldn't catch or kick a ball to save my life. At the time, I had no idea how overtly gay my voice sounded. This was one of the reasons why I quickly earned the nickname faggot at Dover. In physical education class I was always, without fail, the last boy picked when it came to choosing footy teams.

Dad was not home in the evenings because he worked night shifts to get extra pay from loading. But he did phone us from work every night to say hello and check how we were. Until he phoned, I'd put my headphones on because Mum would try to start conversations with me, asking dumb questions about my least favourite subjects.

She'd ask, "How was school?" or "Have you done your homework?"

I'd pretend not to hear her and listen to my favourite album, Madonna's, *Like a virgin*.

"What about your piano practice? Have you done your piano practice?" She'd keep on until I'd explode.

"Look, Mum. I can't hear you with these things on!" It was all I could say after surviving another hellish week at the worst high school in the world. I didn't want to tell my Mum the real reason I was upset. I was too ashamed.

After we swallowed our third West Coast Cooler, Tiffany leaned on me just to stay on her feet. She gave me a peck on my lips and smiled. It was our first real kiss, and it was a blur. "I'm glaaad you came. Yoooou'rrrre my veeeery best friend."

The tiles on the bathroom wall spun around us and we couldn't stop giggling at how wasted we were.

"I think I'm piiissed," I said.

"I think you're shit-faced," Tiffany screamed with laughter.

Even though I was drunk for the first time, I couldn't get Matt out of my head. If he knew I was in the bathroom alone with Tiffany, he'd kill me. Everyone knew Matt had the hots for Tiffany. The next thing I knew, I was in deep shit.

"What the fuck?" Matt grunted when he saw Tiffany and I stumble out of the bathroom, arm-in-arm.

Everyone in the living room just stared, knowing trouble was brewing.

"That's bullshit, mate," Shane said in a thick Islander accent. "You should smash that faggot in the face!"

"You idiots! Nathan and I are just reeeally good friends!" Tiffany slurred her words and grabbed my hand to dance with her, swaying obliviously, side to side. A drunk teenage girl's dance of defiance.

At least no one would think I was a faggot anymore, I thought, as Matt gave me a dirty look from across the crowded room. I mentally prepared for Matt to throw the first punch. But, to my surprise, he went one better than hitting me and did something that stopped Tiffany from dancing.

Before anyone realized what was going on, Matt lunged out the window and hung on by one arm yelling, "I'm going to kill myself!"

Everyone rushed to the window. Matt's face turned red as he struggled to hang on. The fall was over five meters.

"Stop being an idiot!" Tiffany yelled at Matt as he dangled from the windowsill.

Being drunk and hating Matt, I found this chain of events hilarious and burst into a fit of laughter. "Wish he would let go!" I grinned.

Tiffany also burst into laughter and so did Matt's friends.

"Jump! Jump! Jump!" the intoxicated D-Graders began to chant as a joke.

"Stop it!" Anna yelled. "He's going to get hurt!"

"Shane, help him!" Evelyn tried to reason with her big brother.

But Shane was too wasted to care. "Let go, you chicken!" Shane dared.

I saw Anna and Evelyn looking at each other nervously. I think they were the only sober ones in an apartment crammed with drunken teenagers.

"I'm not bullshitting!" Matt screamed as his hand disappeared from the windowsill. Whether he'd meant to let go or not, Matt landed on the concrete car park below. And we all fell silent because he wasn't moving.

"Shit! Get him before the neighbours call the cops!" Tiffany yelled at the boys who followed Shane out the door while the rest of us stared at Matt's limp body on the concrete below.

"We better call an ambulance!" Anna yelled.

"We can't!" Tiffany panicked. "My mum's going to kill me!"

"But what about Matt?" Anna was shocked.

"He could be hurt," I said, suddenly feeling much more sober.

To everyone's relief, Shane returned with Matt hanging off his shoulder.

Matt was limping on one leg and wore a smug expression on his face. "Tricked you!" Matt laughed. He was so drunk he couldn't feel a thing.

Tiffany's tense expression eased when she knew Matt wasn't badly hurt. Or at least, couldn't feel it because he was so wasted.

Shane plonked Matt onto the sofa where Matt soon passed out cold. He didn't even flinch when Tiffany jabbed his shoulder.

"Dag!"

Matt just groaned in response.

For the next hour, everyone talked about how freaky it had been when Matt let go:

"What a loser!"

"Sure, you would!"

Throughout year 8, parties like this became commonplace, always at someone's home while the parents weren't around, or in a park where we could drink unsupervised under the cover of nightfall. It was always the older kids who scored the booze and the younger girls who, strangely, wound up losing their virginity.

Tiffany pressed play on the stereo and the Talking Heads began to sing, *Stop making sense*. Suddenly, it was like nothing bad had happened. That is, until Tiffany blew a thick cloud of smoke at us that stunk. She was holding a fat, rolled-up cigarette that didn't smell like nicotine. I knew it was a joint. Someone, I don't know who, perhaps one of the older kids, must have brought a joint to the party.

"Want some?" Tiffany offered casually.

No one was threatening to flush my head down a toilet bowl.

I wasn't nervous or scared, but drunk and having the best time ever since I'd started high school. So, I put the joint to my lips and took a hit. As I exhaled, the entire living room seemed to sink, and I felt heavier and happier. I offered it to Anna and Evelyn, but they refused, so I passed the joint back to Tiffany.

"Wicked, isn't it?" Tiffany grinned from ear to ear.

I smiled back and we both laughed. But our laughter didn't last.

"Shit! It's the cops!" Shane yelled from the window.

On the street below, a blue and white chequered police paddy wagon parked outside. All the boys ran for it except for me and Matt, who was still unconscious. The girls tried to help Tiffany hide the evidence, throwing empty cans of kids beer and West Coast Cooler bottles into the bin. But it was too late. We were busted big time.

Two constables entered the apartment. They looked sternly at us intoxicated minors, without a parent in sight.

"Party's over," one of the policemen announced in a deep voice just as Matt began to vomit all over the sofa. The police phoned for an ambulance and forced us to sit still in the living room as they wrote our names and parents' phone numbers into a little black notebook.

"Don't give them your real name," Tiffany whispered into my ear.

I don't remember how I got home. I barely acknowledged my parents when I came through the front door. I saw a blurry vision of Mum looking horrified as I walked into the wall.

'He's drunk!" she shrieked.

Dad had to guide me to my bedroom.

"Jesus, Nathan, you're only fourteen years old! What are you doing getting plastered at your age?"

I woke in the morning next to a bucket full of vomit. I had the worst headache of my life, and my tongue was stuck to the roof of my mouth. I was scheduled to have a piano lesson at 9 a.m. Half asleep and half-awake, I could hear Mum apologising to my piano teacher, Miss O'Dwyer.

"I'm very embarrassed for making you come all this way for nothing."

"Please don't apologise, Mrs Jones," Miss O'Dwyer sounded equally embarrassed. "I hope Nathan feels better soon. Tell him to keep up his practice. There's only two more months until his exam at the Conservatorium!"

Mum paid Miss O'Dwyer her hourly fee even though there was no lesson, and she didn't let me forget about it for weeks to come.

TOTAL ECSTASY

1989, FUN LOVE, HORDERN PAVILION

IT HAD BEEN over half an hour since we'd taken the ecstasy. We'd been on the dance floor, explored the carnival rides outside, smashed into each other with dodgem cars, and we still we didn't feel any different.

"I'm having fun, but I'm not euphoric!" Anna complained.

"Yeah, the eckie hasn't done a thing!" Lee agreed.

"Shit, do you think we've been sold duds?" Sarah asked.

"Come on, guys," Evelyn tried to lift our spirits, "Can't you hear what music they're playing?"

Inside the Hordern, the crowd cheered to the authentic disco sound of ABBA's 1970s classic, *Dancing Queen*.

"Yeah, so what if they don't work?" I shrugged. "This is still a great party. Let's enjoy it."

We returned to the dance space where retro DJ Maynard was behind the turntable deck wearing a bright orange Hawaiian shirt and dancing like he was receiving electric shocks from the sound system.

"I love Maynard!" Anna yelled.

"Me too!" Evelyn smiled. "He's totally out-there!"

Maynard's set included *Boogie Wonderland* by Earth, Wind & Fire, followed by KC & The Sunshine Band's *That's the way I like it*. The songs were dated, cheesy, and so tragic that they were cool again and that's precisely why they were so much fun to dance to.

The ultra-cool clubbers were getting into the classic 70s disco sound, and we had so much fun dancing to the daggy music that we forgot about how disappointed we'd been over being sold dud ecstasy pills.

Then DJ Maynard started to play a second ABBA track called *Gimmie, Gimmie, Gimmie (a man after midnight)*, and I suddenly started to feel something. I found myself really, *really* getting into the music. I danced much faster than I had to *Dancing Queen*. Something was happening to my arms. I was inexplicably over-excited to be hearing this song on a packed dance floor with a thousand other grinning faces, all the super-cool and fashionable party people were grooving like professional dancers on the set of a choreographed music video.

"I've always loved ABBA," I yelled in Sarah's ear. "Ever since I was a little boy, I used to listen to ABBA, when I was like four-years-old. ABBA was my first true love before I discovered Madonna."

Now I was sixteen years old, dancing to ABBA with my best friends and six thousand amazing people in the Hordern Pavilion. Suddenly, I realised my arms were floating away. I could no longer feel them! With each breath I took, I felt like I was going to fly. As I moved to the disco beat at an increasing speed, my whole body felt like it was filling up with helium, lifting me up to the lights above. My heart raced.

"Can you feel it?" I asked my friends.

Anna and Sarah laughed intensely.

"I'm fully feeling something!!" Lee grinned.

"It's coming on!!" Simon agreed excitedly and started to dance twice as fast as normal.

"They weren't duds!!" Sarah cheered.

Evelyn smiled at us, yet her face showed she was not happy. Being the only one who refused to try it, Evelyn didn't look like she was having as much fun as we were. She just watched as we started to get very hyperactive.

"It is totally ecstasy!" Anna exclaimed with wild eyes as she gave Evelyn a big hug, followed by Sarah, Simon, Lee, and me.

"I've never been this high before!" I giggled, "It's nothing like being drunk or stoned."

"I love you guys so much!!" Sarah grinned, "You're my very best friends, and you're like my family!"

"Me too!" I felt like I was going to burst with happiness.

"I love you guys so much!" Lee joined in.

We said stuff we'd never normally have the guts to say. Stuff we were too repressed to admit to or would be too self-conscious to say in real life. Yet there was one thing I didn't say about myself. The ecstasy wasn't that strong.

On ecstasy we made friends with complete strangers dancing around us. All it took was to catch the eye of someone who was wearing a big ecstasy induced grin and suddenly you were best friends.

"Having a good time?"

"The best!"

"What are you on?"

"Eckie."

"Me too!"

It was so easy to talk to complete strangers.

A gang of gym buffed men danced near us and I found it impossible to keep my eyes off their muscular bodies. It was like my eyes were glued to their perfectly sculpted chests and toned torsos as they grooved to the disco music. None of them wore shirts, just torn jean shorts, Doc Martin boots, and military dog tag chains.

Anna noticed me looking at them and asked me if I thought they were gay.

"Who?" I played dumb.

"The body boys!" She grinned nodding to the muscle men.

"Probably, but then you have so many straight guys here like Lee, Simon, and me, it's hard to tell." I giggled.

"Yeah, who can tell these days?" Anna laughed.

Evelyn didn't say much as we talked and talked. She just watched us with an expression that reminded me of motherly concern. It was like she was supervising us. Evelyn watched closely as Anna hugged a man who was shirtless and was holding hands with another man.

"Oh my god, I can't believe you're here!" Anna screamed.

"Anna?"

"Guys, this is my horse-riding instructor, Fred!" Anna yelled.

Fred looked stunned to see Anna. He couldn't believe the sixteen-year-old girl he taught to cantor around Centennial Park on Saturday afternoons was now racing around a gay dance party, off her tits on ecstasy with her *high* high school friends.

Fred's partner's face was a mixture of confusion and euphoria.

"What are you doing here?" Fred asked.

"Same thing you are!" Anna beamed.

After dancing non-stop for an hour, Anna, Lee, Simon, and I talked with extreme enthusiasm about what a good time we were having, while Evelyn didn't say a word and Sarah just froze. There was no smile on Sarah's face. It was expressionless. She looked like a zombie. Her eyes were wide and vacant, like she'd seen a ghost.

"Sarah?" Evelyn tugged Sarah's arm, noticing something was wrong. She turned to us and asked, "Guys, what's up with Sarah?"

"Hey, Sarah, are you ok?" Anna tried to reach Sarah. But it didn't work. Sarah continued to sit motionless, like she was having a bad reaction to the pill.

"Sarah!" I shook her gently. "Are you ok?"

She didn't respond.

This cracked through my fuzzy, drug hazed happy view of the world as it dawned on me that Sarah was not right.

"What should we do?" Anna looked alarmed and no longer quite as ecstatic as before.

"I think we should get her to a doctor." Evelyn was concerned.

BALDIES

1987, THE BONDI BOTTLE SHOP

A YEAR AFTER TIFFANY'S party, where I first got drunk, I soon became the one who bought alcohol for my school friends. The first time I did it was from a bottle shop near Bondi Beach. To look adult, I wore my very best pair of stone washed denim jeans and a 100% Mambo t-shirt. I put gel in my hair and styled it like I was James Dean.

Inside the bottle shop, I grabbed a six-pack of West Coast Cooler and a 4-litre cask of Tropicana wine cooler from a wall of refrigerators at the back of the store. A video surveillance camera recorded my every move and under the watchful camera was a sign that said, *"You must be over 18."*

My armpits sweated as I plonked the booze onto the counter. I didn't open my mouth because the guy behind the cash register would see my braces and it would be obvious I was four years shy of being over 18. I looked older than most boys my age, having grown a foot taller than the rest in my class, but I still had pimples and was skinny as a surfboard. I knew my height alone wouldn't be enough to convince the shop assistant I was an adult. That's why Tiffany had made me a fake ID. She used her Mum's home-office photocopier and some carefully applied Liquid Paper to make a copy of her late father's birth certificate look like it was issued in 1969.

But the guy behind the counter didn't even look at me as he scanned the items. "Nineteen-ninety-five," he said but seemed more interested in a football match playing on a small TV behind the counter.

Almost trembling, I handed over the cash and the sale assistant put the booze into a brown paper bag.

Hiding around the block from the bottle shop were Tiffany, Sarah, and Evelyn. They cheered when they saw me exit while carrying a bag full of booze. We got drunk in North Bondi Park under the cover of nightfall before going to the Blue Light Disco at the surf lifesaving club. The police ran Blue Light Discos as no-alcohol zones. That's why we got drunk before we went in to dance until midnight.

Some older kids from school were also drinking alcohol in the park, including Evelyn's brother, Shane. "How can you drink that shit?" Shane scoffed at us for drinking West Coast Coolers. "That stuff is for baldies, man!"

"What's a baldie?" I whispered to Evelyn.

"Means you haven't grown any hair...down there," Evelyn whispered back embarrassed.

The seniors didn't touch West Coast Coolers. They were into harder stuff, like spirits: Jack Daniel's and Jim Beam. That's why I bought a bottle of Jack Daniel's when I returned to the same bottle shop a few weeks later. I didn't want our gang to look like a bunch of baldies.

Since I'd already gotten away with buying booze without being asked for ID, my confidence levels were high. I put on a deep voice and made small talk with the shop assistant to distract him from how young I was. "Had a hard week at university," I lied, as I plonked a bottle of Jack on the counter.

"What do you study?" the assistant asked, disinterested.

"Journalism," I lied. Truth was I hoped to study journalism one day, maybe even become a news reader. Buying booze forced me to think about what I wanted to do when I left high school. Something I could not wait for!

Each time I returned to the bottle shop, I created a whole new personality and potential career to go with it. Pretending I studied law one week and medicine the next. At least I sort of knew what I wanted to do when I was over eighteen, which seemed like forever away. I hated high school so much. Perhaps that's one of the reasons I was so easily led to get wasted on the weekends.

DANCE IT OFF

1989, FUN LOVE, HORDERN PAVILION

"SARAH CAN YOU hear me?" I was yelling by this stage. We each tried to snap Sarah out of her catatonic state. But she didn't budge. It was like we weren't even there. It was as if she'd disappeared from her own body.

"Guys, we've got to get her to a doctor, fast!" Evelyn pleaded.

"No!" we all protested. We were all scared that our parents would find out what we'd done.

Desperate, I took Sarah's hand. "Let's just dance it off!" I suggested. It was the only solution that made sense at 3 a.m. Saturday night/Sunday morning, high on ecstasy for the very first time. I led Sarah to a spot on the floor that was not too crowded. The floor was filled with dance party people having the best time of their lives, dancing with pure joy while Sarah just stood there, unable to move.

"Try and enjoy it," I urged Sarah. I grabbed her arms, moving them back and forth, trying to bring Sarah back to some form of reality. This only made her look like she was going to cry. So, I tried a different approach, and I gave her a big hug and felt her relax in my arms.

The rest of the group was looking at her to see if Sarah was okay.

"I love you guys!" Sarah said, nearly crying, unable to handle the intensity of the emotions she was feeling. Lost for words, she hugged each one of us; one by one. Lee gave me a concerned look as Sarah hugged him and wouldn't let go. Over Sarah's shoulder Lee mouthed the words, *Is she ok?* and pointed to Sarah's back.

I nodded that she was, relieved.

"It's cool," Sarah finally announced. "I just got over-emotional, but it's okay. I feel like I'm part of the party again. I just felt very distant before."

With Sarah smiling again, we danced until dawn and left the party at 8 a.m.

"I'm glad you guys are ok," Evelyn said, exhausted.

"Yeah, I can still feel it but it's not as strong now," Lee said.

"I'm no longer peaking," Anna agreed. "But I'm extra alert, like I'm able to hold a conversation but I'm really, *really* tired."

"I'm totally aware that I've just had the very best time of my entire life!" Simon exclaimed.

We couldn't stop talking about what an amazing night it had been and how high we still were.

"How do we get home?" Evelyn asked, weary.

"Let's walk through the park!" I grinned, still wide-eyed.

We walked towards my parents' home through Centennial Park, dressed in our acid house dance party inspired clothes, stinking of sweat and cigarette smoke. We collected more than our fair share of raised eyebrows from the early morning joggers and cyclists exercising in the park that Sunday morning.

Once we got back to my parents' place, the girls collected their stuff and shared a taxi home with Lee and Simon. My parents were hospitable and blissfully unaware.

They had no idea what we'd gotten up to the night before.

OVERPROOF

1987

IN SCIENCE CLASS, our lab had six four-seater tables. The popular kids made sure they all sat together. Across from me were two girls from Bondi Public School, Melissa and Tammy. They giggled and whispered to each other and paid no attention to me. The seat next to me was empty.

Lee was the last boy to turn up to class. When he saw the only empty seat was next to me, he sighed, and the rest of the boys cracked up.

"You've got to sit with the faggot!" chuckled one of them.

"That's enough!" Mrs Templeton scolded him.

Lee dragged his feet towards the empty seat.

During class, Melissa and Tammy turned their attention from the chemical elements to Lee's Chinese features. They whispered mean insults just loud enough for Lee to hear but quiet enough so that Mrs Templeton couldn't. The girls cracked each other up.

At the end of class I caught Lee wiping away a tear. I felt bad for Lee. I knew how much it sucked and felt to be called names. So, I stood up for him. "Shut up, you vicious dogs!" I snapped.

Melissa and Tammy's jaws dropped.

"Fucking faggot!" Melissa fired back.

"Cujo!" Lee spat at Melissa.

"What's that? Some stupid Chinese swear word?" Tammy shrugged.

"You're Cujo, the vicious dog from Stephen King's movie — the one with rabies," Lee teased.

Most of the class overheard and burst into laughter.

Both girls were left speechless and folded their arms annoyed that their classroom antics had worked against themselves.

That's how Lee and I became mates. He even taught me how to swear in Cantonese and I taught Lee how to get drunk by inviting him and Simon to Evelyn's infamous party. Not that I could later remember much of it.

The sky turned purple as we walked in a pack to Evelyn's party. It was Saturday night. As we made our way to the party, we passed by Dover High carrying a bottle of Bundaberg Gold Overproof Rum in a brown paper bag.

"Hey! Let's check out what Dover's like at night!" Lee yelled as he ran through the school gates with Tiffany. I chased after them and the rest followed. It was the first time any of us had been excited about going to this school in our lives. At night, the city skyline shimmered in the distance from the playground. Our laughter echoed across the empty quadrangle and bounced off the brick walls.

"At night, the view from school is so beautiful," Tiffany said like she was seeing the beautiful view for the very first time.

"It's hard to notice during the day," I reminded her and twisted open the bottle of Bundaberg.

"Wow! It has 57.7% alcohol," Simon said.

"That's heaps more than Jim Beam," Tiffany nodded.

I took a swig, and it tasted like fire, burning my throat as it went down. I tried to extinguish the fire and washed away the poisonous taste with Coca-cola. Tiffany, Lee, and Simon also took a shot while Anna and Sarah watched. They refused to try it.

"Yuck!" Lee looked like he was going to be sick and spat out the rum.

"Hey! Don't waste it!" Tiffany grabbed the bottle and took a long sip. Without even flinching, Tiffany swallowed a mouth full and washed it down with Coke.

Lee and Simon shook their heads amazed.

"Steady on!" I took the bottle off Tiffany. "Leave us some!"

After sharing a few more sculls, our voices grew louder, and the sensation of the cold night air was numbed by the alcohol. At this hour, the school and the city lights were ours. I drank what I thought was an equal amount to my friends. However, I actually ended up swallowing half the bottle on my own. The burning sensation that tasted so horrible at first had become a mildly pleasant sensation travelling down my throat by the tenth scull.

Lee and Simon had to drag me to the party. It seemed so funny that I couldn't walk without their assistance. I thought they were having as good a time as me until my mouth filled with saliva, and I spewed all over the neighbouring garden to Evelyn's apartment block.

"Whoops," I apologised before drifting into an oozing state of blackness.

The next morning, I woke up in a bathtub not knowing where I was. My jeans and t-shirt had dried vomit splatters. I got up slowly because it hurt to stand. I was in Evelyn and Shane's apartment; their Dad was away for work and the place was a mess. There were older kids from school passed out in front of the TV and empty beer cans everywhere.

"You're alive!" Evelyn looked happy to see me. She was the only one awake, watching music videos on the TV and munching corn flakes. "You missed the best party!"

I couldn't take another step without feeling like I was going to hurl. I had no choice but to phone my dad to come pick me up. I was so sick and in big trouble!

Dad wasn't angry with me the way I'd imagined he would be. He spoke softly as he drove me home, "You shouldn't be doing this. Not at your age."

I said nothing as I lay on the back seat trying not to throw-up. I kept my mouth shut, fearing if I opened it only vomit would come out.

"You're going to end up a no-hoper if you keep this drinking up. Your mother's going to be disappointed. We hoped you learnt your lesson about drinking from the last time. When she sees what you've done this time, she's going to worry you'll end up like your grandfather."

"What?"

"I never wanted you to know this, Nathan, but you've left me no choice. Your grandfather was a drunk. I grew up dirt poor thanks to my Dad's drinking and gambling. During the Depression, we nearly lost our home. When I was growing up it was nothing like what you're used to. No Atari or TV in my bedroom — we had nothing!"

Dad turned off Oxford Street to where we lived near Centennial Park. He parked in the driveway of our four-bedroom town house. Thanks to my parents, I had the luxury of growing up in a well-to-do upper-middle-class neighbourhood. Dad had done well for himself considering how he had grown up. He sounded angry as he switched off the engine. "No more pocket money, Nathan. It is time you grow up and learn how hard it is to earn money for yourself. Get your own damn job!"

"Had a good spew, Nathan?" Shane yelled at the top of his lung first thing Monday morning in the crowded school stairwell.

All the senior boys cracked up laughing as they pointed at me. Everyone at Dover Heights High, including the teachers, heard him. My cheeks felt hot with embarrassment as I pushed through the students in the stairwell. But it was nowhere near as embarrassing as when I was called faggot.

"News travels fast!" Lee shook his head.

"Oh my god," Evelyn said, picked up her pace. "How *shameful*!"

"Why did you get so wasted?" Anna asked.

"I didn't mean to get that wasted," I answered defensively.

"Sure, man. You're a total alcoholic. Everyone knows it!" Simon giggled.

"I swear, I'm never going to drink again," I vowed as we entered the classroom for English period.

During class, I didn't listen to a word Miss Hillstone had to say about the book we were meant to be reading, Aldous Huxley's *Brave new world*. I was thinking about what everyone at school must think of me. At least they weren't calling me a faggot anymore. As humiliating as it was to have everyone think I was an alcoholic it was better than them thinking I was a homosexual.

AFTER EFFECTS

1989, THE MORNING AFTER FUN LOVE

I SPENT SUNDAY SOUND asleep and woke up to see the sun setting. At dinner, I was too tired to chew my food and didn't feel hungry at all. My jaw was sore from chewing gum all night on E.

"Not hungry?" Mum was surprised.

"Normally, you eat like a horse," Dad commented. My Mum and Dad were clueless about what was going on.

I shrugged, unaware why I wasn't hungry. My ears were ringing. I returned to my bedroom and turned on the radio to listen to Triple J FM. I had to study. There was a math test on Wednesday. I opened my 3-unit textbook and stared at a page of trigonometry. A few minutes passed before I realised I wasn't doing anything except staring blankly at the page. It was like my brain was disconnected. I sat motionlessly at my desk, barely hearing the radio, facing an open page of triangular diagrams, looking like a zombie.

"My mind's not in gear," I muttered and closed the textbook.

At school, Anna overheard Evelyn telling Elizabeth what we had gotten up to at the Fun Love party. This was bad news because Elizabeth was our elected member for the student council, and she was kind of uptight, the biggest teacher's pet.

"Are you serious?" Elizabeth gasped when Evelyn told her she thought we were becoming drug addicts. The more details Evelyn revealed to Elizabeth about what had happened at Fun Love, the more Elizabeth became convinced that we had a drug problem. "Should we tell their parents?" Elizabeth asked.

"You mean dob on them?" Evelyn frowned.

"Or should I alert the Principal?"

"No way! It's their decision."

"But it would be for their own good."

Luckily for us, Evelyn convinced Elizabeth not to tell anyone, for now.

The next night, instead of doing homework, I phoned Anna. For some reason, all I could think about was the weekend. "It was the best night!" I reminisced.

"Except for that bit when Sarah went all weird," Anna spoke softly.

"That was so freaky."

"She was catatonic!"

"Do you think ecstasy is dangerous?"

"You mean like Elizabeth does?"

"Who cares what she thinks."

"Evelyn told me Elizabeth thinks we're drug addicts."

We both cracked up laughing at the idea.

"As if." I giggled. "All we've done is taken a pill. Once! How does that make us drug addicts?"

"I know! But it got me thinking. Don't you want to know for sure that we're not going to suffer any long-term damage by taking it?"

"I guess," I said. I hadn't really considered this before. "What are you saying?"

"I was thinking of calling that toll free number for the Australian Government Drug Offensive Hotline to see if they know. I want to be sure we'll be okay."

"For real?"

"Yes! I'd rather know than not know."

I said nothing.

The idea of phoning a government drug hotline freaked me out.

"No way. What if they tape the call? If you're serious, make sure you do it from a pay phone so they can't trace the call."

That's how, after school, Anna and I embarked on some extra-curricular 'homework'. It was a secret research assignment whereby we phoned the hotline to get more information about drug taking. We used the Telecom pay phone outside Dover Heights High. Anna put a 20-cent coin in and dialed. We wanted to keep this conversation as anonymous as possible.

"Hi. I have a *friend* who took ecstasy." Anna tried to put on a mature voice, but she sounded like the Queen of England. I had to cover my mouth to suppress a sudden urge to laugh. "Shush!" Anna waved at me while she covered the receiver. "They'll think it's a prank call!"

I put my ear to the outside of the phone handle to hear the voice on the other end.

"Are you seeking advice on how to help your friend?"

"I want to know if anything bad can happen if you take ecstasy."

"It can cause several symptoms, insomnia, jaw tension, and overheating. To be honest, the drug hasn't been around long enough for any hard data to indicate if there are long term effects. If you — *your friend* — is taking ecstasy, they are experimenting with their life. I'm sure there are serious and negative side effects from this drug. We just don't know what they are yet. I can send you more information if you give me your name and address."

Anna slammed the Payphone handle back into the cradle and looked annoyed by what she'd been told. "Well, that didn't help at all!"

"Told you, it's not like they're going to tell you it's good to take drugs."

"I know. I just want to know more. Why can't they just tell us the truth? I want to know if I am going have any long-term problems from taking that one little pill."

But on Wednesday, when we had our first math test for year 11, suddenly I began to care. The first question was about the cosine rule.

I spent five minutes racking my brain for the answer, but I couldn't remember how to solve the problem. So, I moved on to the next question, an algebra equation, which I couldn't answer either. Next it was fractions, and the same thing happened. It was like each question was way too hard — or I had studied the wrong chapter from my textbook.

Nothing like this had ever happened to me before. I normally aced these exams. When the same thing happened on the next five questions, I looked up to check how the rest of the class were doing. All their heads were down, pencils were scrawling answers, and calculator keys were being punched in a race against the clock.

Except for Lee. He caught my eye and shook his head.

I checked that Mr Johns wasn't looking and mouthed, *Fuck!* I tried to do the remaining questions but could barely solve half of them. There was another fifteen minutes left on the clock. I tried every question again, twice, without success. I waited for the exam to be over, feeling stupid and nervous. I knew that this was the worst I'd ever done on a test in my life.

Before the exam ended, Anna looked up and shrugged. She gave me a look and it was like I could read her mind. She likely felt the same about the test, as I did: *No idea!*

Everyone agreed that the test was tougher than anyone in the class had been prepared for, even Elizabeth, who stayed home all weekend to study for it.

"How hard was it?" Elizabeth shook her head once we left the classroom.

"I think I failed!" Anna sighed.

"Me too!" Lee and I agreed.

I knew the problem wasn't that the questions were too hard. It was because the dance party took up the entire weekend when I should have been studying. Also, my brain wasn't as sharp as it once was after taking the ecstasy pill. I could feel the difference in my alertness. I promised myself I would never combine coming down from E with any future HSC pre-qualifying tests.

"I'm so exhausted," Anna sighed on the school bus home.

"Me too," Lee agreed.

"I just feel so bored," Simon said.

"Me too," I muttered. For some reason, it was an effort just to say those two simple words. I was totally disinterested in everything.

During the rest of the week the only thing that made me come alive was talking about what we did at the dance party and how good ecstasy was. It was better to focus on that than knowing I failed the first math test, 5% of which would contribute to my final HSC mark. That was so depressing.

By Thursday, I still couldn't get my mind in gear. I knew this wasn't normal and it made me anxious. I started biting my nails and tapping my legs constantly under the school desk during class.

By Friday night, I decided to phone the Australian Government Drug Offensive Hotline again, hoping that maybe they'd know what was happening to me. This time, I called them from my parents' home phone. I didn't care if they could trace the call. Clearly, I wasn't thinking right. But I had to know why I was feeling so weird and over everything since I had taken the E.

A man answered and asked how he could help.

I told him what I'd done on the weekend and how I was feeling now.

He told me, "When you take a drug like ecstasy, your body puts out three days' worth of energy in a space of just several hours. Your body is catching up. You're coming down. What you're feeling will pass, provided you don't take any more ecstasy."

RESTRICTED PREMISES

1988, BONDI JUNCTION

B Y YEAR 10, Tiffany and I had developed our own special going-out routine. On Friday night, we would meet up at Bondi Junction train station dressed to party. We would buy a hip flask of Jim Beam and a bottle of Coca-Cola from the local bottle shop. Together, we'd scull the bourbon in the seclusion of a high-rise construction site and giggle as we passed the Jim Beam back and forth until the bottle was empty, and the world was spinning. We'd wash the fiery bourbon down with Coca-Cola in less than twenty minutes.

At fifteen-years-old Tiffany and I were *over* just getting drunk. It had become so try-hard. We were ready for something more adult. After putting up with school all week, Friday night was our time to let loose.

"Want to check out what Kings Cross is like at night?" Tiffany asked all excited one day.

"Let's do it!!" I was drunk enough to think it was a great idea.

We headed to the train station and bought two tickets to the red-light district. It didn't bother me that Tiffany collapsed onto the metal escalator steps as we travelled down into the railway tunnel. I giggled at the commuters waiting on the platform, because they gave us disapproving looks. It was a look of, *You should know better at your age!*

"What?" Tiffany grinned, oblivious.

"Nothing."

"What's so funny?"

"We're freaking everyone out!"

Tiffany just pointed and laughed at the adults giving us dirty looks.

Ten minutes later, we stepped off the train onto the platform at Kings Cross.

After ascending to the top of the escalator Tiffany tugged my arm. "I have to pee."

I waited outside the ladies toilet as Tiffany entered. I leaned against the wall, trying not to look wasted.

There was a gang of westies hanging out on the seats nearby, wearing flannelette shirts, sheepskin boots, and sweatpants. They had seriously bad haircuts. Who in their right mind would think that having a mullet or short haircut with a long rat's tail was a good look? I thought they were so ugly compared to us stylish Eastern suburbs kids. I tried not to look at them in case they tried to pick a fight.

Tiffany raced out of the toilet. "A girl is shooting up in there!"

"For real?"

Tiffany nodded, looking more sober than before as we climbed the steps towards street level.

Outside, the night was alive with bumper-to-bumper traffic. A gang of rough looking kids drank near the gutter. Prostitutes stood in strip-club doorways. And there were people like us, out for a good time.

Within a minute of walking along the main street, a strip club doorman dressed in a black and white tuxedo blocked our path. "Want to see a show?" he asked encouragingly.

"No thanks." I looked away. I knew he was trouble.

"Forty dollars. It's the best show in town!" The doorman wouldn't let up.

We kept walking.

The doorman sidestepped in front of us. "Ok. For you, thirty dollars." His voice was like gravel.

"Not interested," I tried to sound strong.

"Twenty dollars, that's my last price." He backed away.

Tiffany looked at me with a twinkle in her eye. "Okay." She smiled.

"Are you serious?" I asked.

"Come on!" Tiffany giggled. "It'll be hysterical!"

"Listen to the lady." the doorman patted my shoulder. "You're going to love it, boy!"

I followed Tiffany and the doorman through an entrance outlined in pink neon lights. The sign left nothing to the imagination as it flashed, GIRLS, GIRLS, GIRLS. Tiffany was so drunk, she laughed hysterically as the doorman led us through a dark corridor covered with red velvet wallpaper. I felt scared of where we were going but was too afraid to let it show. The corridor ended with another security door. Above it was a sign that read, RESTRICTED PREMISES.

A fat, middle-aged man sat behind metal bars and a cash register.

"Twenty dollars apiece," the doorman told the fat man.

"Twenty each?" Tiffany raised her voice. "I thought you said twenty dollars for the two of us to get in."

"Love, I'd lose my job if I let you in for ten dollars apiece!"

"Twenty each! No way man!" Tiffany grabbed my hand and ran for it.

I stumbled after her.

"What a rip off!" Tiffany laughed as we escaped from the strip club.

In a drunken haze, we stumbled through the red-light strip, past cafes and sex shops. We stopped to rest at a water fountain shaped like a sphere.

"So glad he didn't run after us," I said as I tried to catch my breath.

"Hey, do you want to see if we can get into a real night club?" Tiffany's eyes were wide with excitement.

"Okay!" I was more eager to try that than a strip club.

"Opposite the Coca-Cola sign is a night club called the Oz Rock Café." Tiffany smiled.

"I've heard about that place on the radio. It sounds cool." I nodded.

We walked towards the giant glowing neon Coca-Cola billboard flashing above William Street. Across the street, under the red glow it told us all to *Enjoy*, as we joined a line of people waiting to get into the massive five-story hotel.

To our surprise, we got in without any questions.

Inside, the music was so loud I had to scream into Tiffany's ear, "This is awesome."

The dance floor was completely empty apart from the smoke and flashing lights. It was surrounded with men in tight jeans and colourful pastel shirts. Women wore revealing dresses with too much make-up. Tiffany took my hand to head onto the dance floor. We danced and cheered like we owned the nightclub as the DJ played our favourite song, *Never gonna give you up* by Rick Astley. We were a million miles away from being just mere high school students. It was the best place to be. No one to tease me there.

The alcohol started to wear off as we moved our bodies to the beat, but the natural-high grew stronger. I couldn't believe that we'd made it into a nightclub at fifteen years old! It was our biggest achievement to date.

Unfortunately, both our mums expected us to be home by midnight. They thought midnight was a reasonable curfew for someone of fifteen and a half years of age. We stayed on the dance floor until 11:45 p.m. and left just as the club was beginning to get full. The atmosphere was becoming wild inside the club with cheers and sounds of people having fun. Tiffany and I caught a train back to Bondi Junction.

As our carriage rattled home, I decided I wanted to return to the dance floor. "I'm going to get a part-time job," I announced proudly.

"Why?" Tiffany looked at me like I was joking.

"To do this again, I'll need more money."

THE EXCHANGE

BEING TRAPPED IN high school meant only having a miniscule budget to live off. Mine consisted of the pocket money my parents gave me for a lunch allowance, plus cash gifts from relatives that I saved from my birthdays and Christmases. I wasn't the type of kid who could go without eating several times during the day, so, without a part-time job, my weekly allowance would have been gone in a single Friday night.

At recesses and lunch, I lived off junk food. Chicken burgers and crumbed drumsticks were my favourite. But what I became most famous for was the day I ate four rainbow Paddle Pops in a single lunch break. After all, I was a growing teenage boy. That was my excuse for being a pig. Going to Kings Cross on Friday nights forced me to be more responsible and motivated me to get a part-time job after school.

I got employed at Baskin Robbins. My pay cheque was *totally* worth the humiliation of serving 31 flavours of ice cream in a seriously humiliating pink and brown uniform three nights a week on Camp-bell Parade at the Bondi store.

Tiffany was luckier by comparison. She got extra pocket money for doing filing at her mum's real estate office after school.

Thanks to our part-time jobs, we were able to return to the dance floor of Oz Rock Cafe. When we went out, Tiffany and I split our going-out expenses 50/50. We shared a hip flask of Jim Beam, which cost us $5 each, a bottle of Coca-Cola for $1.50. The Oz Rock Cafe cover charge cost $7 to get in, plus we had to pay student concession return train fares at $1.50 each. A single night out could cost us around $15.00 each. In 1988, this was a small fortune for most fifteen-year-olds. But it was worth it. Since we'd discovered what was out there outside of high school, staying home on the weekends was for losers.

Under the glittering mirror balls of the Oz Rock Cafe, Tiffany yelled in my ear, "We dance funkier than any of the adults do!"

As if to prove Tiffany right, a middle-aged guy approached her to say, "I like the way you move."

Tiffany ignored him and rolled her eyes. The older guy couldn't see she was making fun of him. He had a thick gold chain around his neck and smelt like he showered in grandpa cologne: Old Spice.

It surprised me when adults tried to talk to us. We were so obviously plastered and underage. For some reason, this guy didn't get it that Tiffany wasn't interested in him. We were there to *dance*.

"So, Doll, would you like to come back to my place for some action?" he asked seductively.

Tiffany stopped dancing and looked at me in horror.

We both burst into laughter.

"Are you serious?" I was drunk enough to have the courage to yell at the sleazy old man.

"What are you? Some kind of perve?" Tiffany looked him up and down with disgust. "Gross, man!"

"Hey, take it easy!" He backed away and disappeared into the crowded dance floor.

After he was gone, I said to Tiffany, "This place must have a pick-up rating of 11 out of 10."

"Do you want to try somewhere cooler?" Tiffany flicked her bleach blond fringe. "Like Oxford Street, maybe?"

I looked at Tiffany, unsure. All I knew about Oxford Street was that it was for gays.

"No way! Tiffany… I don't think that's a good idea."

"Why not? Oxford Street is where the most fashionable clubs are in Sydney, stupid!"

"I don't know…"

"Come on! What are you afraid of?" Tiffany couldn't understand why I was so uncomfortable at the idea of going to a gay club.

So, I spelt it out. "What if the kids at school find out?" I couldn't handle being called a faggot all over again. Not now that I was nearly a senior.

"Who cares what they think?" Tiffany tugged at my hand. "Let's get out of this place. It's full of creeps!"

"Okay. On one condition: we don't tell anyone where we've been."

"Deal."

We left the Oz Rock Cafe and walked along Darlinghurst Road towards Oxford Street. On our way, we passed The Wall. I tried not to stare at the teenage guys waiting on the street for cars to come by and pick them up. Some looked like they were the same age as us. It was the middle of winter, and one boy was wearing only a singlet. He looked like he was freezing. He reminded me of that Willesee TV interview I had seen when I was a kid, about Greg *the junkie*. But Tiffany didn't seem to notice them. She was more excited about going to Oxford Street.

"I want to see if we can get into The Exchange! It's the place to be seen!" Tiffany was bursting with excitement. "When Culture Club toured Australia in '84, Boy George went there! We've got to see if we can get in! It'll be so cool!"

Tiffany had been the biggest Culture Club fan at primary school when she was eleven years old. She insisted that Boy George wasn't gay. We used to fight about it. She was heartbroken when she found out he was not just gay, but a junkie. Based on what I'd seen on TV by the age of fifteen, I thought all gay guys were junkies.

Uncomfortable thoughts filled my head as we got closer to Oxford Street. Even Tiffany got more tense than usual. "I hope they let us in!" she said nervously.

I kept thinking that perhaps going to The Exchange wasn't such a good idea. My palms began to sweat, and I wondered what the gay guys in the club would think was the real reason we were there? What if they thought I was one of them? My heart was racing.

Tiffany stopped to light up a cigarette. "You should light one too," she told me. "It'll make us look older."

I took a smoke from the pack. "Maybe we should talk about something only adults would, when we get near the doorman," I suggested, as I blew a puff of smoke. "You know, so they don't think we're underage."

Tiffany took my advice and as we approached the entrance to The Exchange Hotel, she said something that she thought sounded adult enough to impress the towering doorman. "Did you hear Angela had an abortion?" Tiffany raised her voice for effect.

"I can't believe she doesn't practice safe sex!" I played along and lowered my voice to sound older. At Dover, we'd recently had to sit through an hour-long sex education talk by counsellors for HIV/AIDS. I didn't think what they said had any relevance since I was still a virgin.

With cigarettes hanging from our fingers, dressed all in black, talking about abortions and AIDS, Tiffany and I looked and sounded as over-eighteen as we could. Without waiting to be let in, we just waltzed past the muscle-bound doorman and made it in without him flinching a single muscle.

Inside The Exchange, it was completely dark. It took a second for our eyes to adjust to the purple UV neon black lights that made everything white glow in the dark. Our smiles shined so bright they could have been seen from space.

"Woo hoo!" Tiffany screamed.

"How easy was that?" I exclaimed.

"No, it wasn't!" Tiffany folded her arms. "We're not your average fifteen-year-olds you know?"

The bar was crowded with men. Most looked like male models, wearing the latest fashion: 501 Levi Jeans, shiny black Doc Martin shoes, and tight white t-shirts, with braces. The few women in the club also wore very similar fashion to the men or wore flannelette shirts. Only these women weren't westies, they were lesbians who also looked like handsome boys with short haircuts.

"You were right! This place is way cooler than the Cross!" I smiled not feeling as uncomfortable being in a gay bar as I'd imagined I would. Suddenly, I didn't care what the gay guys inside The Exchange thought of us. The music was different to the Oz Rock. It was faster and more electronic.

The dance floor was only a tiny stage, about a meter wide, opposite the bar. It was crowded with people dancing and trying not to fall off as the DJ spun MARRS's *Pump up the volume*. Tiffany and I got up to dance and it felt like all the men at the bar were watching us. My heart was racing. But on the outside, I acted cool and pretended not to notice. I danced closer to Tiffany to show them I was here with a girl! I was not gay!

Tiffany leaned towards me. "I think this crowd is 50/50, half gay and half straight — but cool like us."

"Just like us." I nodded but, for the first time, I wasn't so sure this was really the truth. Why else would I feel so turned on by the tall blond man dancing behind Tiffany? He kept looking me in the eye and I couldn't stop looking back.

As the DJ changed the tune to Depeche Mode's *Strange Love*, it suddenly made sense why all the boys at school called me a fag. Somehow, they knew. They had all known before I did.

For the first time, I accepted in my mind that the boys at school were right about me. I belonged to the gay half of the crowd.

Still, there was no way in the world I would tell anyone, especially Tiffany. It didn't matter that she was the one who'd dragged me to a gay bar, nor that she'd been my best friend since we were six years old. There was no way I could tell her because Tiffany truly believed I was straight, like her. I wasn't sure how Tiffany would react if she found out. I didn't know what she would do. What if she turned her back on me? I couldn't handle that. Or what if Tiffany told someone? What if they found out at school? They'd all start teasing me and picking on me for being a fag all over again.

My life wouldn't be worth living. There was no way I could tell anyone — ever. I'd have to keep this secret until the day I died. That's why I kept on dancing and pretending that Tiffany was my girlfriend.

"They're all giving you the eye!" Tiffany yelled in my ear. I followed Tiffany's gaze towards a group of men watching us on the dance floor and nearly had a heart attack. She was right! They were all looking directly at me. At my ass — and they were being totally obvious about it.

I guess I had changed a lot since I used to spend Friday afternoons staring at my ugly reflection in the mirror. My braces had come off, my teeth were perfectly straight, and I no longer had acne. Plus, I was one of the tallest boys in my year. I had dressed well and spent over an hour doing my hair in the bathroom mirror. I was sort of good looking now, for a fifteen-and-a-half-year-old.

Tiffany laughed in my ear over the booming music. "I keep looking back at them, going *ha ha, you can't have him, he's mine!*"

I gave Tiffany a peck on her cheek to emphasise to the good-looking men in the gay bar that I was with a girl! "They can look all they want." I pretended to be completely uninterested in the gay guys watching me. The truth was that I was more than interested. I just couldn't do anything about it. Not with Tiffany, *my girlfriend,* dancing by my side. My eyes wandered back to the handsome blond man dancing by himself behind Tiffany's shoulder. His eyes met mine for a second then he pretended not to be looking.

That night, after I said goodbye to Tiffany following our curfew, I waited for her to get safely inside her home. Once she was in, despite my parental-imposed midnight curfew, I raced back to Bondi Junction and jumped into a taxi alone instead of going home.

"Where to?" the driver asked.

"Oxford Street," I said feeling more paranoid than I ever had in my whole life. My heart pounded, full of nervous energy. I knew going to a gay bar at 11:23 p.m. on a Friday night, alone, was probably dangerous for a fifteen-year-old. Mum and Dad would be expecting me home in less than thirty minutes. But I didn't care. This was something I had to do. I was running on instinct.

When I got out from the taxi, the line waiting to get into The Exchange was much bigger. I joined the queue and waited anxiously, tapping my Doc Martins, feeling extremely self-conscious and scared someone from school might see me by accident.

A smirk appeared on the statuesque doorman's face. He recognised me from earlier in the evening when I had been with Tiffany; now I was alone, and he nodded for me to enter yet again. Inside, I felt nervous standing among a bar packed with gay men. In the dark smoky atmosphere, I spotted the same blond guy who'd caught my attention earlier.

He smiled when he saw I was standing by myself and pushed through the crowd towards me. "Hey, I'm Andrew," he introduced himself. His eyes were beaming. The black of his pupils were much larger than normal and his smile was angelic, perfect, like a Michelangelo fresco. Andrew was wearing faded blue jeans, a white t-shirt, and a black leather jacket.

"I'm Mark." I decided it was best to lie about my name. I couldn't risk Andrew, or anyone at The Exchange, knowing who I was or how old I really was. But I didn't need to worry because Andrew wasn't interested in conversation. The next thing I knew his body was pressed against mine, and our lips were locked as he kissed me in the middle of the bar. All I could hear was the chorus from Kylie Minogue's *I should be so lucky* playing in the background as we kissed.

The guys in The Exchange cheered at the DJ's song choice. Gay guys loved Kylie, even more than regular, respectable *Neighbours*-watching Australians did.

Unfortunately, it was midnight, and my luck was running out.

"I've got to go." I broke away from Andrew's embrace.

"What?" He pulled a disappointed puppy like expression.

"I've got to leave!" I was anxious and excited from having my first kiss with a boy.

"What's wrong?" Andrew grabbed my arm. "Can I have your number?"

I made up a fake phone number, along with my fake name, for my pretend Prince Charming and, like Cinderella, fled at the stroke of midnight. I got home before 12:30 a.m. and freaked out because both my parents were waiting up for me.

Mum was not impressed. "You're late." She frowned.

"There were no buses," I lied. At least I hadn't come home drunk. I never told a soul about what I had done on the weekend.

DOUBLE LIFE

THE FOLLOWING WEEKEND, Tiffany insisted on going back to The Exchange because she'd had so much fun. There was no protest from me.

We repeated what was to become our new routine: we returned to the same construction site, got wasted sharing a hip flask of Jim Beam, washed it down in less than ten minutes with a bottle of Coca-Cola, caught the 380 for a blurry bus ride along Oxford Street, waltzed passed the doorman like he wasn't even there, and then danced like we owned the club until 11:45 p.m.

By then the alcohol would have worn off and our curfew would be up, so we would catch the 380 back home again where I would say goodnight to Tiffany with a big hug and a kiss.

Then came the bit Tiffany didn't know about: my new routine. I'd sneak back to The Exchange by myself. One night, it didn't take long for me to make eye contact with another handsome man standing at the bar. Earlier in the night, this man had been watching me when I was on the dance floor with Tiffany. Now he could see I was alone, so he made his move.

"Want to come back to my place?"

"Um…"

"I live a block away in Darlinghurst." He smiled warmly.

"Sure," I agreed, even though I wasn't sure it was a good idea leaving with a stranger. But I knew I was ready to try more. It wasn't like I could do this with one of the boys at Dover. I'd be killed! The stranger didn't say much as we walked through the backstreets to his place. He stopped outside a federation-style sandstone terrace and put a key in the door. Within seconds of closing the front door, he grabbed me and kissed me frantically as he pulled my t-shirt over my head.

"Hey, go easy!" I said uncomfortably. "It's my first time."

"That's what they all say!" He grinned, thinking I was joking. It was happening way too fast! We rubbed our bodies together, his hands reached into my pants aggressively. Being my first time, it didn't take long before the joke was on him. I was a virgin, in a hurry, and it was past my curfew. Once we were done, all I could think about was getting out of his place as fast as I could. For me, the fun was over. It was almost 1 a.m. I had to get home. I imagined Mum and Dad yelling at me for coming home so late. The thought of HIV didn't even enter my mind. I was more concerned about getting home on time, so my parents didn't freak out. I collected my clothes off the polished floorboards, pulled up my jeans and didn't care about how disappointed he was.

"Can I see you again?" he asked.

I wrote down a fake phone number and wondered if I was developing a split personality.

As I caught the 380 bus home, I feared someone from school might have seen me walking alone on Oxford Street at night or, worse, seen me leaving The Exchange with a man. I lived in fear that I would be caught, not just by my parents, but by someone from school. There were older boys in year 12, like Evelyn's brother, Shane, who had a car and their P-plates. At school, they bragged about how they drove up and down Oxford Street on weekends screaming faggot and went out poofter bashing.

It they'd spotted me, I'd be dead.

STRAIGHT GUY ON THE EDGE

THERE ARE SOME things in life you never expect to change, and when they do, you know nothing will be the same ever again. That's how it was when Tiffany told me her mother was getting remarried and they were moving to America.

"No way!" my voice went up an octave.

"Hate my mum! She's ruining my life."

"When are you leaving?"

"Next month. You're the first person I've told. Please write to me every day."

"You can call me, too, if you get rich!" I tried to make Tiffany laugh because it sounded like she had been crying. Suddenly, I had a hard time imagining my life without my imaginary girlfriend.

The last night I saw Tiffany, we went to a pizza bar in Bondi. We didn't even get drunk. We just talked about how much we meant to each other. How we'd never forget each other and made a pact to stay friends for life!

When it came time to saying goodbye, we held onto each other tightly and for a long time. Neither of us wanted to let go. We had practically grown up together and known each other for most of our young lives. If I'd been heterosexual, we probably would have gotten married.

"You better not forget me!" Tiffany sobbed.

"I won't!" I said feeling like a piece of me was missing suddenly.

"I love you." Tiffany kissed me goodbye and entered her home.

As I walked home alone, I looked at my watch; it was 10 p.m. I decided to go to The Exchange. As usual, I had no trouble getting in by myself. At fifteen and a half years old, I had become a regular. Without Tiffany, I would never have discovered it. She was the coolest girl friend. We had done everything together. Well, almost.

Inside the bar, it didn't take long before my eyes zoomed in on a tall, well-built man standing by the cigarette vending machine. Without meaning to, I caught his eye and our eyes locked. We checked each other out, then he looked away. I was disappointed; maybe he wasn't even gay? Or perhaps he was like me, when I went out with Tiffany, a closet gay acting straight: *a straight guy on the edge.*

And there it was: I realised that I was truly on my own! No more security blanket girlfriend. I decided it was time for me to make the first move, so I approached him.

"Got a cigarette?" I asked

"Sorry, buddy." He shook his head.

"Oh." I attempted to hide how embarrassed I felt at being rejected in a gay bar for the first time. "Thanks anyway." Humiliated, I went to the opposite end of the bar and was thinking about leaving, until I noticed the same guy standing behind me.

He had followed me across the bar. This made me extra nervous, and excited. I really did need a cigarette to calm down. As if reading my mind, he held out a pack of Winfield Blue cigarettes and offered me one.

"Thanks." I took the cigarette then realised Tiffany had my lighter. Now that she was gone, so was my light. I felt stupid and obvious asking, "Do you also have a light?"

He smiled and lit my cigarette. The light illuminated his rugged square jawline, blue eyes, and blond hair; classic good looks. "I just ran out when you asked. I've been trying to quit but you just gave me a good reason to buy another pack."

"Sorry."

"I'm not." He held out his hand for me to shake. "I'm Campbell."

"Mark." I tried to smile convincingly as I shook Campbell's hand.

"So, Mark." Campbell eyed me up and down, "Are you old enough?"

"Yes!" I answered almost too defensively. Without hesitation, I said I'd just turned seventeen. Up-close, it was more believable than pretending I was over eighteen. Eighteen was two and a bit more years away. "How old are you?" I asked Campbell.

"Twenty-one."

"And…are you gay?"

"Why else do you think I would be here?"

"You just don't seem gay. I mean, you don't look or act like gay guys are supposed to."

"Right. So how are gay guys supposed to act?" Campbell moved closer and pressed his body against mine. His mouth tasted of beer and cigarettes. "Want to come home with me?" Campbell asked.

"Sure." I played it cool, even though I knew my parents would be expecting me home any minute. But I reasoned that this was my time. It wasn't like I could do this in the school playground.

Outside The Exchange, Campbell hailed a taxi.

"Where to, sir?" an older taxi driver asked politely.

"Manly." Campbell fastened his seatbelt.

Shit! I panicked. Manly was an hour's drive away from where my parents lived.

The ride seemed to take forever. The taxi driver asked for more than just directions. "Australian men, you have big dicks, correct?" He had an accent, but I couldn't tell where from. I was too shocked at his question.

Campbell gave me a puzzled look, checking he hadn't misheard the question. But seeing the amused expression on my face, Campbell realised he had heard right. "Excuse me?"

"Aussie men have big dicks?"

I burst into laughter and Campbell grinned.

"Mate, we sure do."

Campbell lived in an apartment block that faced Manly Beach. Once we got through the front door, it was completely different to what had happened the previous time I went back to that other guy's place in Darlinghurst. Campbell wasn't like that. He showed me into the living room, offered me a drink, and opened the balcony door. I could hear the waves crashing on the shoreline as I checked out his apartment. On the fridge was a set of photos held in place by smiley face magnets. In one of them, Campbell had his arm around a young woman. They were holding a baby and had wedding rings on their fingers.

"Are you married?"

"Divorced. Married my high school sweetheart. But it didn't work out."

"What happened?"

"For starters, I'm a poof. What do you think happened? I worked out I was gay a tad too late. So, I came out. Just couldn't hide the truth from her — or myself."

"Heavy."

"It's all good now. We're still friends and I have a beautiful baby girl – Emma. She lives with her mum. But enough about me, let's get back to you, young man." Campbell took me to his bedroom where we undressed each other.

I stayed at his place for the whole night. It never occurred to me to call my parents to let them know I was okay. I didn't think I needed to, because I felt safer and more secure than I ever had in my whole life. Also, I was too distracted under the covers.

The next morning, Campbell lit up a cigarette. "I knew I would meet someone special before I left."

"What?" I was half asleep.

"I'm moving to Canberra next week." Campbell blew a cloud of smoke.

"You're kidding." I couldn't hide my disappointment. "Why?"

"Got a new job," Campbell told me. "I've recently been promoted."

"Oh." I couldn't believe it. I pictured Tiffany boarding a plane with her mum and soon-to-be stepdad, and now this! "Can we stay in touch?"

"Sure. That would be swell." Campbell ran his hands through my hair. "Damn, you're gorgeous. What did I do to deserve meeting you?"

I gave Campbell my real phone number before I left. But I didn't tell him my real name. I wasn't ready for that.

I caught the Manly ferry to get home. As the boat crossed Sydney harbour early Saturday morning, I could see my high school building perched on top of the hills of Dover Heights. In the distance, a jet flew across the sky. It was a reminder of what I faced on Monday morning. Tiffany was no longer in the country, and I would be back at Dover without her.

As the ferry chugged past the Opera House towards the Bridge, it closed in on the tall buildings of Circular Quay. I knew I'd fallen in love. Or at least felt something close to how I'd imagined love would feel. It didn't matter that I had a headache from sleep deprivation or that I'd missed my curfew. I felt incredible, like I had grown up. Overnight.

I stepped through the front door of my parents' house the next morning at 8 a.m. I figured Mum and Dad would be asleep because the place was dead silent — until Mum ran down the stairs.

"Where have you been?" Her face was ghostly white.

"Err... I was out with friends," is all I could offer.

"That's a lie!" Mum looked like she hadn't slept all night either.

I tried to get past her, but she pushed me back.

"Where have you been?" she demanded. "Your father is out there right now driving around looking for you!"

"Dad's out looking for me?" I almost giggled at the thought of my father driving around looking for me, but I controlled myself not wanting to make the situation any worse. "I was with Tiffany."

"Stop lying! We called Tiffany's parents to see if she knew where you were — Tiffany said she hadn't seen you since 10 p.m.! So, where the hell have you been?"

There was no way in the world I could tell her the truth. I knew Mum couldn't handle it.

"Tell me!" Mum demanded.

I ran for the upstairs bathroom and locked the door. In the mirror, I saw my reflection. There were purple-red marks all over my neck. Giant love bites. "Shit!" I cursed as Mum continued to yell from the other side of the door.

"Your father's reported you missing to the police. We're going to look like the worst parents in the world now you've come home!"

I hadn't meant to cause this much upset. But as Mum yelled, I became furious. I was the one who'd just lost their best friend! Plus, the love of my life was also leaving town!

"You're never allowed out again Nathan. That's it!"

I looked back at my reflection with pure dread. Not because of what Mum had said. It hit me that my mum had phoned Tiffany last night to find out where I was! That meant Tiffany would know I hadn't come home last night! I started to panic, wondering what Tiffany would think I had done. Suddenly, I was glad Tiffany was on a plane bound for America; otherwise, I'd have to think of a cover story real fast for last night.

"You're lucky you weren't killed!" Mum cried. "You're only fif-teen-years-old! What were you thinking? We thought you were more responsible than this! You should be ashamed of yourself! I don't even want to know what you got up to!"

When Dad came home later that morning, he said just one thing, "You must really hate us.' He was so angry with me, that was all he could say.

On Monday morning, everyone at school paid out on me when they saw the marks on my neck, thinking they were from Tiffany.

"Were you attacked by a vampire?" Lee joked.

"Gosh! That is some farewell present," Evelyn teased.

"Ooooh!" the others crooned suggestively at the love bites from Campbell.

They were still just as visible at school as they had been when I'd come home and given my Mum a nervous breakdown. I was happy to let my friends think they were from Tiffany. It built up my reputation as a heterosexual.

On the school bus later, everyone yelled to be heard over the engine. All the kids were excited to be going home. In contrast, Anna noticed I was unusually quiet.

"You okay?" she asked me.

"Yeah."

"You seem down."

I didn't answer and continued to stare out the bus window.

"You're missing her, hey?"

"What?"

"Tiffany?"

"Oh, yeah. Heaps."

It was true, I did miss Tiffany, but it wasn't the reason I was quiet. I hated that I had to pretend Campbell didn't exist. But what choice did I have? I had to act like nothing had ever happened even though it was the only thing I could think about.

I got a postcard from America fourteen days after Tiffany left:

To Dear Nathan.

How are you? I miss you and hope that you miss me too. I hope you're having a great time. Say hello to your parents and everyone at school. I'm in L.A. right now, but by the time you get this I'll probably be in San Francisco. We are going to compare L.A. to San Fran and see which one we like the best and then move into a home. I do miss you and I'm sure that I'll see you soon. I'll write again and let you know where I've ended up.

Luv Tiffany.

P.S.
I hope you have as much fun going to nightclubs and exploring different parts of town with your friends as you did with me.

xoxoxo

I never got a phone call from Campbell. Even though I waited by the telephone, he never called. I stayed home on Friday night for the first time in a long time and wrote back to Tiffany while listening to songs that reminded me of her, like The Cure's, *Why can't I be you?* and *In between days*.

Tiffany and Campbell were the two most important people in my life, and they'd never gotten the chance to meet each other. Not that I wanted them to. I would die if my two worlds ever collided.

FAKE ID

TOWARDS THE END of year 10, there was nothing left in my life but homework. My report card proved it. My grades were above 80% for math, English, history, science, economics, and art. I was in the top 10% of the A-Grade class. But my report card wasn't perfect. Every teacher wrote comments that concerned my parents, saying I was *"easily distracted"* or *"distracted the class"* or *"wasn't performing to my full potential."*

With Tiffany in America, my other school friends became more important to me than ever. I was lucky to have them to hang out with. When we graduated from year 10 with our School Certificate, Evelyn encouraged the gang to go clubbing to celebrate.

"Clubbing?" Anna looked unconvinced. "That sounds so try-hard."

"How would you know?" I got defensive.

"Yeah," Evelyn backed me up. "You've never done it!"

"But you know, it will be harder to get in because it's school holidays," I warned. "We need to make you guys' fake IDs."

On the last day of school, we headed to the school library and photocopied the fake ID Tiffany had made me a few years ago. This was because Anna and Sarah looked their age: sweet sixteen. We each applied Liquid Paper to the multiple copies of the same fake birth certificates and made ourselves nineteen years old on paper.

We put the fake IDs to the test that weekend. I took my friends to the Oz Rock Hotel. There was quite a line to get in.

"I hope they let us in!" Sarah whispered to me.

"They'll let us in — you'll see," I whispered back to Sarah, as we lined up to get into the Oz Rock Cafe.

The bouncer simply eyed us up and down. "Got any ID?" He sounded like he knew we weren't old enough.

"Yes." I fumbled for my wallet and pulled out the tattered fake birth certificate I had been carrying around for the last two years. Strangely, this was the first time I had put it to the test.

The bouncer looked at it with confusion. "You got to be kidding!" The bouncer laughed. "Next!" He motioned for the couple standing behind us to step up.

Our group turned away, humiliated.

"Oh my god, that was so shameful!" Evelyn looked shattered.

"You should have seen your face!" Anna giggled, "You were all like…" Anna made her face look like she was constipated.

"Shut up!" Evelyn slapped Anna's arm playfully.

"What are we going to do now?" Lee folded his arms disappointed.

"We can try another club," I suggested, not ready to give up on our mission to celebrate surviving four years at Dover Heights High. "I used to go to another club on Oxford Street with Tiffany. I think you'll like it."

We headed to The Freezer on Oxford Street, Darlinghurst. The Freezer was so cool it didn't even look like a club from the outside. There was no sign on the door to identify it was a nightclub. Its exterior was painted black and that was it. I think that was the point — to keep out any undesirables.

This explained why at 9 p.m. no one was waiting outside to get in. But this didn't stop us. In fact, it helped because it was too early for the club to have a bouncer on the door. It was the type of club that came alive at 11 p.m. We seized the opportunity, walked in, and paid the cashier $10 each. The only people in the tiny club were a barman and the DJ playing to an empty dance floor.

"Oh my god, this place is so cool!" Evelyn didn't care we were the only ones in the club.

"Where are all the people?" Lee looked at me, confused.

"It's totally dead!" Anna laughed.

"It'll come alive, just wait," I acted cool.

We took over a booth at the back of the club next to the dance floor and shared one drink between us. It took another forty minutes before more people arrived. Upon seeing it was virtually empty apart from us, they left. Bored of waiting for something to happen, we got on the dance floor as the DJ played Womack & Womack's, *Teardrops*.

An hour later, the club filled with the local inner-city crowd, the type of people who hung out at Paddington Markets on Saturday afternoons and constantly wore dark sunglasses on Sundays.

"This music is so cool," Anna yelled to Evelyn. "Thanks for convincing me to come! I was so scared this would be like that horrible party you dragged me to at Tiffany's when we were in year eight. Remember how terrible it was before it got raided?"

"That was the worst!"

"How cool are the people in this club?"

"The coolest people!"

"They dance so fast!"

None of us appreciated what it took for the inner-city Paddington crowd to dance so energetically. It took more than alcohol or pot.

A RATTY NEW YEAR PARTY

L EADING UP TO New Year's Eve for 1988/89, colourful billboard posters were stuck to every lamppost along Bondi Beach, Paddington, and Oxford Street. They were promoting A RATTY New Year, New Year's Eve party, (RAT was short for the 'Recreational Arts Team'). It was going to be a massive party for twenty-thousand people to be held at the Royal Sydney Showgrounds. It was being talked up on Triple J FM, as the place to be this New Year's Event the event of the decade.

Everyone in our group decided they wanted to go. The problem was there were no more tickets on sale. The only way to get a ticket was to line up on the night when the final thousand tickets would be released.

Evelyn, Sarah, and I were determined to be there. We volunteered to line up at the Showgrounds at midday to make sure we got tickets and planned to meet up later at my parents' house around 9 p.m. before the party.

"Shit!" Sarah cursed when we saw the length of the line outside the Showgrounds. It stretched from the ticket gates for an entire block. Waiting on the footpath were hundreds of people with the same last-minute idea.

"Looks like a thousand people are already ahead of us!" Evelyn complained as we joined the end of the queue.

After running out of things to talk about as we waited in line for an hour, Sarah said out of the blue, "I wonder if we'll get offered acid or ecstasy. Aren't that what dance parties are all about? Taking drugs?"

"No!" Evelyn looked annoyed. "They're about dancing!"

Looking at the crowd waiting in the line, I knew Sarah was right. They looked like the biggest druggies on the planet. It was a parade of young people with bright coloured hair, tattoos, shaved heads, mohawks, leather studded bracelets, torn fishnet stockings, Doc Martin shoes, and tank tops. Evelyn, Sarah, and I stood out because we were so clean cut. We were pathetic teenyboppers compared to everyone else waiting in the line. I began to wonder why I had never been offered acid or ecstasy before when I went clubbing with Tiffany. Had we been that uncool?

According to the newspapers, ecstasy was all around the Oxford Street clubs. The Sydney Morning Herald's 'The Good Weekend' magazine, that my Dad read, claimed that Sydney's trendy social elite were all taking this new designer drug called ecstasy in clubs and at warehouse parties. I had read the article with great interest sitting in front of the TV watching *Video Hits*.

The article described how wonderful and potentially dangerous, even deadly, this new psycho-active love-drug was, how it was *"an integral part of the club scene"*, how *"the summer of 88/89 was being called the 2nd Summer of Love"*, and that *"in London it was estimated that more than 1 million people had tried ecstasy"*. When I read The Good Weekend article it made me feel concerned. Why hadn't we been offered ecstasy?

At 6 p.m., the ticket box opened, and the crowd surged with excitement. A full-scale riot nearly erupted as the people who'd waited all afternoon rushed forward, desperate to get their last-minute tickets. The surge only lasted a short time because the ticket box shut again to control the crowd and we went back to waiting.

By 9:30 p.m., Anna joined us in the line. She was all dressed up in black and white polka dots, ready to party. Evelyn, Sarah, and I were still dressed in the clothes we'd been wearing since morning. "I went to your place, but your mum said you hadn't been home all day. So I came here to find you! I can't believe you guys have been waiting here all day!"

As each minute passed, we were squashed against the other sweaty bodies surrounding us, as even more people turned up hoping for last minute tickets. At 10 p.m., the gates opened for the clever people who'd bought tickets in advance. They rushed for the gates, and we got caught in the riptide of bodies. A girl ahead of us fainted and was soon carried away by paramedics who were on stand-by.

Finally, we reached the turnstile and got our tickets. We jumped up and down with joy until we realised that now we had to line up to get out! It was two hours until midnight and we had to meet Lee and Simon. They were probably waiting for us at my parents' house. How awkward. When we got back to my home in Bondi Junction it was nearly 11 p.m. We got changed and were ready to head back to the Royal Showgrounds.

My Dad was so good. He offered to give us a lift back to the Showgrounds. When we returned, the queue outside the gates had tripled in size.

"Nathan, I don't think your mother would approve of you going to this. It looks like mayhem!" Dad said, concerned.

My friends thanked Dad for giving us a lift and hopped out of the station wagon. "Thank you, Mr Jones." They were overly polite.

"Take care. Look out for each other," Dad sounded distracted as he scanned the queue outside the gates.

"Thanks, Dad. Don't worry," I assured him. "We'll be fine!" I slammed the car door shut.

"Your Dad is so cool!" Sarah was amazed.

"Yeah, mine would never let me out of the car if he saw where we're going!" Evelyn chuckled.

Beyond the gates, house music blasted and thousands of people mingled while dressed in amazing outfits: tight glitter bra-tops, hot pants, jean shorts, black cycle shorts with red braces, leather jack-ets, feathers, and fluorescent-combinations. It was like they had just stepped off a music video set. There was a Ferris Wheel, dodgem cars, and a giant jumping castle! Our group held hands as we raced through the party, checking out every bit of it. Inside, the Hordern Pavilion was packed with thousands of people dancing to the sounds of the Jungle Brothers, *I'll House You*.

There were drag queens, gay guys, lesbians, and people from all backgrounds singing the words. The music was relentless, a mix of mechanical beats with flashing lasers and strobe lights bouncing off giant mirror balls. Within ten minutes on the dance floor, we were drenched in sweat. It was so hot that even the walls were perspiring.

"Nathan?" I heard a familiar voice call. "Oh my god. Is it you?!"

I spun around and couldn't believe it. Standing in front of me on the packed dance floor was Michael from my old primary school, shirtless. No longer was he the porky kid Tiffany and I had shared cigarettes with at primary school. Now he was lean and athletic, and all the girls were looking at him.

"Michael!" I went to shake his hand, but Michael just gave me a big hug, like I was a long lost relative.

"Wow! I haven't seen you since we were twelve years old!" Michael grinned from ear to ear. "I can't believe you're here doing exactly the same thing we are!"

"I know!" I couldn't believe it either and was surprised when Michael wouldn't let me go. He just kept on hugging me like I was his lover. He introduced the girl he was with, "This is my girlfriend, Sally!" Michael grinned at me like he was going to burst with excitement.

"Are you on E?" was the first thing Sally asked.

"E?" I didn't get what she meant at first, then I realised she meant ecstasy.

"No, I don't do drugs!"

"Seriously, you should try it. It's the best!" Michael grinned as he sweated heavily. Michael acted so overly friendly when I introduced him to my friends that he seemed gay. Or was it the drugs making him act gay? I wasn't on drugs and was pretending to be straight. The 80s were a confusing time to grow up.

I wondered what ecstasy was like but I was reluctant to try it because of all the bad stories attached to this drug. Yet watching Michael dancing happily with his arms in the air and hugging us, it didn't seem as bad as what the newspapers had made it out to be.

At 4 a.m., there was a performance by Grace Jones in the Royal Hall of Industries. Grace began her show by spinning around in a leather swivel seat high above the masses on a giant podium. She opened with, *Slave to the rhythm*, and the audience erupted with cheers and applause. Even though we weren't old enough to be that familiar with her songs, we all agreed she was amazing and mesmerising.

The next morning, on the first day of 1989, we joined the hordes of people streaming out of the Showgrounds wearing dark sunglasses as they spilled onto Driver Ave. We left the RAT party at sunrise.

"Wow!" was all any of us could say of the experience.

"I feel like we've discovered something big!" Anna commented.

"I can't wait to go to another one!" I said enthusiastically.

YOU'RE A MINOR

ON NEW YEAR'S Day, I decided to ring Campbell's old phone number, hoping whoever answered might have his new number. A guy answered and gave me the number for Campbell's mother. It took me until the next day to work up the courage to dial the number. I was bored out of my brain and tired of listening to my parents reminisce about the good old days with my grandparents who were visiting from Queensland. I took the portable phone and locked myself into the bathroom to make sure I had some privacy.

"Hello?" Campbell's Mum sounded posh.

"Er, hi. You don't know me. I'm a…friend of Campbell's." My heart pounded. "Do you have his new phone number? I want to wish him a Happy New Year."

"And you are?" she sounded suspicious.

"Mark," I lied. "We met before he moved to Canberra."

"I see." She sounded kind of sad as she gave me Campbell's new phone number. I wrote it down and stared at the piece of paper for a minute and wondered if I really wanted to do this. It was embarrassing that Campbell had never called after our night together. Maybe he didn't want to hear from me, I thought with disappointment.

I dialed the number regardless. With each ring, intense feelings rushed back that I hadn't felt since the night I'd spent with Campbell, along with the shame I'd felt when my parents had gotten angry the next morning.

"Hello?" Campbell answered and instantly I was glad I phoned him.

"Guess who?"

"Hello?"

"It's me."

There was a long pause. "Mark," I reminded him of my fake name.

"Mark!" Campbell's voice warmed up. "Where have you been?"

"Here."

"Where? I rang that number you left me three times before I realised you slipped me a fake one, or I wrote it down wrong?"

"What number did you ring?"

Campbell recited my parents' phone number off the top of his head. "I memorised your number. When you spend a night like that with someone it's not easy to forget. Each time I rang, a woman told me that 'there is no Mark living here.' Are you a closet gay? No, let me guess. You're married?"

"That was probably my mum. Don't worry, I'm not married or nothing." It was time to tell the truth. "My name isn't Mark. It's Nathan. And I didn't just turn eighteen, I'm sixteen."

"I see," Campbell's voice went quiet. "I should have guessed."

There was a long-distance silence, and I was conscious my parents were paying for it. "I rang to say Happy New Year! How have you been?"

"It's been tougher getting settled than I thought. Leaving friends, plus I couldn't stop thinking about you. What did you say your real name was?"

"Nathan."

"It's funny. I thought you gave me a wrong number on purpose. I really wanted to see you again. But that's out of the question now."

"Why?"

"You're a minor."

"What are you saying?"

"You're not old enough to be a consenting adult. Shit! I can't believe you're only sixteen."

"We didn't do anything wrong. It wasn't like you forced me!"

"Doesn't matter. I... I can't believe I'm having this conversation." Campbell let out a shaky breath over the receiver.

This was not going how I hoped it would.

"Who cares?" I said, "I'm not going to tell anyone. I wanted it to happen. Can't we be…friends?"

"I guess so," Campbell's voice trailed off. "But we can't…you know…"

THE BLACK PARTY

1989, JANUARY

TWO WEEKS BEFORE the school holidays would end, another dance party was advertised. Black and white billboard posters promoted a new dance party to be held at the Hordern Pavilion called the Black Party. The poster didn't give away any further details other than where to get tickets and what DJs were playing.

It was just the distraction we needed to take our minds off the end of summer holidays and the start of the dreaded HSC.

I pleaded with Mum to give me an advance on next month's pocket money as I'd used up all my money going to the RATTY New Year.

"But, Mum! Why can't I have $40 now? I'm starting my HSC this year and won't be able to spend my pocket money because I'll be studying all the time!"

"That'll be the day! Maybe you can learn how to save some money." She knew me too well. Eventually, she gave in, as did my friends' parents.

The next day, we spent a sunny afternoon walking up Oxford Street to find the places where the tickets were on sale. They were only available at places we'd never heard of before, like The Bookshop, Folkways Music, and the Oxford Hotel.

We found the Oxford Hotel at Taylor Square. It was a few blocks up from The Exchange and was a gay leather bar. None of us had the courage to enter. This should have been our first warning that the Black Party was not going to be anything like the RAT party.

"Hmmm," Sarah said, likely thinking what we were all thinking.

Except for Simon, who said, "Come on. Let's go in!"

We all laughed awkwardly.

"Yeah, you probably come here all the time!" Sarah teased.

None of us had the guts to go in, so we crossed the road to the next venue selling tickets, which sounded harmless: The Bookshop. Upon seeing the window display of rainbow flags and book covers with semi-nude men, it was Simon's turn to make a joke, "Lee, this must be where you get all your books from!"

"No. But I bet you do!" Lee fired back.

Again, none of us had the guts to go in and buy tickets. It should have been our second warning. We only had one venue left to check-out: Folkways Music store in Paddington. It looked harmless enough. It was a specialty music store that sold furniture and jazz records. Evelyn and I collected our friends' money and went in since we looked the oldest.

A plump older man behind the counter gave us a strange look when I asked for six tickets to the Black Party. For a minute, I feared he was going to ask for ID, but he didn't. "Enjoy," he said with a cheeky grin.

Outside, Evelyn and I both let out a sigh of relief after he'd taken our money and handed over the tickets.

After much discussion about what we should wear, we agreed it was obvious, we should dress all in black for the Black Party.

As we walked to the Showgrounds the day of the event, I grew excited at the sound of house music echoing through the summer night air. But something was missing as we approached the gates: it was 10:30pm and there were no people in sight.

"Are we too early?" Anna asked, confused.

"Uh-oh!" Lee smirked when he saw we were not alone.

Beyond the wire gates was a morbidly obese middle-aged man with a grey beard, dressed in red high heel stilettos, fishnet-stockings, ballerina tutu, black lace corset, blond wig, and a tiara.

"Oh — my — God!" Evelyn stopped dead in her tracks.

"Is this a Rocky Horror Picture Show theme party?" Simon snickered.

As we handed over our tickets at the turn-styles, we soon learned that we had gate crashed an annual gay and lesbian leather community event. There were people of all shapes and sizes squeezed into every sort of leather and rubber outfit conceivable. People were dressed in uniforms like policemen and nurses. Forget high school, we were in for the education of a lifetime. Gone was the carnival vibe of the RAT party. The theme of The Black Party was sexual, and we were seriously out of place, and we knew it.

On the dance floor, we saw a man who looked like Arnold Schwarzenegger, wearing only a dog-collar and being led on a leash by an equally muscular man who was naked apart from a pair of black Doc Martin boots and a leather G-string. Nothing was left to the imagination. I was turned on by many of the sights I saw, but couldn't let it show as I continued to act straight with my high school friends.

My friends were speechless at the sights around them.

I became paranoid that one of the guys I'd made out with at The Exchange may be among the crowd and would recognise me. What if they came up and kissed me? Or acted like they knew me? How would I explain that away? This situation was not good! My thoughts were racing. I became anxious just being around all these gay men dressed in leather with my school friends by my side.

Anna spotted Michael and Sally. They weren't dressed in leather either. Like us, they looked disappointed by the Black Party crowd.

"Can you believe this party?" Michael grinned.

"It's full on!" I nodded.

"We should make the most of it." Michael shrugged.

"Be careful what you wish for," Anna warned. "I think making the most of it around here could mean getting spanked!"

"I'm going to need a little help to enjoy this party," Michael said as he eyed the leather-clad crowd. "Nathan, do you want to go halves on an E?"

I looked at my friends and could see the concern in their eyes. "No," I said reluctantly. "Thanks."

"Cool," Michael shrugged and went to find a dealer with Sally.

We went outside to get some air and sat on the concrete steps at the entrance of the Hordern Pavilion and watched the sights: middle-aged men in black leather chaps with their white ass cheeks exposed, lesbians in flannelette shirts even though it was the middle of summer, and a few people like us ready to dance all night looking terribly confused.

"We're not going to tell anyone about this are we?" Lee joked as a girl and guy approached us. They were both dressed in black rubber costumes that had flashing red LED lights.

"Having a good time?" the girl asked.

"Yeah." It was obvious from our monotone response what a bad time we were really having.

"I like your outfit," Anna made small talk.

"Thanks, doll. I made it myself. I'm Mini. I'm a design student at the College of Design in Paddington. That's my boyfriend, Graham."

"We're off our tits!" Graham cheered as he sucked on a lollipop.

"We're on E. Have you tried it?"

Our faces filled with curiosity.

"No," Anna was the only one who had the guts to admit it.

"Wow! You must try it! It's unbelievable! I can't believe you're here and haven't tried ecstasy! Oh my god, Graham, these poor people haven't tried ecstasy! They're at a dance party and not on eckie! Can you believe it? What's wrong with you people?" Mini couldn't stop talking. Nor did she wait for Graham to respond to any of her questions before she asked another one. "Ecstasy is perfectly safe you know! Why haven't you tried it yet?? Seriously, what are you afraid of? You should do it! It feels like a six hour long orgasm!"

We all couldn't help but laugh.

After Mini and Graham left, Anna turned to me. "Maybe we should take Michael up on his offer."

"Are you serious?" I was surprised Anna of all people would be interested to try ecstasy.

"Why not? Let's see what it is like."

Out of everyone in our gang, I expected Anna would be the one who would object most strongly to doing it, after all those years of refusing to drink alcohol or mull up. The rest of our group were appalled. They were all looking at Anna like she'd gone temporarily insane.

"Are you for real?" Evelyn folded her arms, "You'll end up becoming a drug addict like Michael and Sally!"

"I don't think Michael is a drug addict," I said.

"Yeah," Anna backed me up. "Michael just takes ecstasy at dance parties. It's not like he does it every day of the week!"

"Guys, think about it. Is this the sort of party where you want to run around and hug everyone?" Lee pulled a face.

Anna ignored our friends. "Come on, let's find Michael to see if he can get some."

It didn't take much for her to convince me. I was easily led. Anna and I tried to find Michael and Sally on the dance floor, but it was impossible. It was a sea of men dancing with men and women dancing with women, all to thumping house music like some kind of alternate reality.

We watched a couple of female belly dancers spray something from a can onto a cotton bandana. They tied the bandana into knots and put the knots in their mouths to suck on whatever it was they'd sprayed on. They looked blissfully happy.

"Weird things are going on at this party that we have no idea about!" I yelled into Anna's ear.

Later, we found Michael dancing with Sally near the ten-foot-tall giant black-box speakers.

"Did you score any Es?" I yelled.

"Can't find any," Michael sighed.

"Hey, maybe that girl, Mini, or her boyfriend knows where we can get some ecstasy," Anna suggested.

So, we wandered back through the dance floor but couldn't see them.

"It looks like everyone here is on something!" Anna commented.

I plucked up the courage to ask a group of older men dressed in leather chaps, "Do you know where we can get some ecstasy?"

"Sorry." They looked at me suspiciously.

Each person we asked gave us the same look, like we were from another planet. It became embarrassing, so we gave up asking. No one revealed where they had gotten their ecstasy from and none of them tried to take advantage of us teenyboppers, who obviously had no idea what they were doing at a leather community event.

We left the Black Party the opposite of high.

It was 3 a.m. when I stepped through the door. I tried to be quiet and not wake my parents and grandparents who were staying in the guest bedroom. Now that I was sixteen and a half years old, my parents didn't give me a hard time about staying out late. They were comfortable knowing who I was out with. They trusted my friends and I wouldn't get up to any no good, as my mum would say.

As I crept to my room, the phone rang. It gave me a heart attack. It sounded like a car alarm going off in the middle of night. I raced to answer it. But it was too late, the entire house, including my grandparents, woke up and realised what time I had come home.

"Guess who?" It was Campbell.

"Nathan, who is it?" Mum called from the hallway.

"It's...Tiffany!" I lied. "She's calling from the US."

"It's 3 a.m. in the morning. Doesn't she know there's a time difference?" Mum told me off as Campbell yelled into my ear, "I miss you so much!"

"Me too," I confessed with a whisper. I couldn't believe he had finally called after all this time.

"I really, *really* miss you." He sounded drunk.

I hadn't expected to hear from Campbell again, but I was happy to, although also alarmed. After being out all night at a hardcore leather party, I was unsure what it meant to be gay.

"I think I love you," Campbell sounded tired and confused.

"Me too," I whispered. Even though I had only spent one night with Campbell, I hadn't thought about anyone else that way since, or gone back to The Exchange to pick up and get off. No one could have compared to Campbell, even if he said we couldn't have sex because I was a minor.

"I don't know what's wrong with me," Campbell slurred his words. "I can't stop thinking about you."

"It's been the same for me, too."

As I said this, all I could think about was what my grandparents must think about me getting phone calls in the middle of the night. I could imagine them thinking *In my day this would have never happened.*

The concept of a teenager had not even been invented when they were my age. I wondered what they must think of the person I had grown up to be. Devil's spawn probably. If only they knew the truth. It would send them to an early grave. My grandparents were very religious. They went to church every Sunday. Thank God my Dad was an atheist. Maybe he wouldn't flip out if he found out my secret.

"I want to see you again," Campbell yelled through the phone.

"Me too!" I became excited.

"But we can't!!" Campbell cried.

SENIORS

WHEN WE BECAME seniors at Dover, all the other groups I used to consider to be more popular than ours seemed to be talking about us, about how we went to gay dance parties and clubs on Oxford Street during the holidays.

"Aren't you scared you'll catch AIDS?" Elizabeth asked Evelyn as we lined up for class. Her voice was filled with disgust. I looked at Anna and Sarah who rolled their eyes, overhearing the conversation.

"I can't believe how unenlightened and bigoted everyone is at this school," Anna complained as we sat down in the uncomfortable red plastic chairs.

"They're just jealous," Sarah said.

In English class, after Miss Hallston welcomed us back to Dover, she gave us a reality check.

"For the next 2 years, all of you will have to knuckle down and study hard. I can't stress this enough. The next 2 years of your life will go by very fast! Before you know it, you will be sitting in a chair for your final High School Certificate exam. My advice is to put in all the effort you can upfront, to give yourself a chance to compete against every other student in this state for a place at university, if that's your goal."

Travelling on the school bus, heading home, Anna pointed out the window with excitement and said, "There's another dance party on at the Hordern!"

The poster on the bus-shelter advertised a new party called Fun Love. It was on a Saturday night, the 11th of February at the Hordern and all our favourite DJs were playing, like Tim Ritchie, Peewee Ferris, and Maynard.

"We have to go!" Evelyn exclaimed.

Elizabeth, who was sitting in front of us, spun around with a dumbfounded expression on her face, "Do you think a dance party is worth risking your HSC?"

"Yes!" we all answered in unison, then burst into laughter.

"I can't believe you want to go to another one, especially after what I heard you guys saw at the Black Party!" Elizabeth had gotten all the gory details from Evelyn about what we had done on our summer holidays. "I can't understand why you'd want to be around those sorts of people. It sounds demented!" Elizabeth spoke with an air of superiority.

"So uncool," Lee said under his breath to us, ignoring Elizabeth's attitude.

We had far bigger concerns; like what we were going to wear.

"I'm going to dress totally acid house for this party." Anna smiled.

"I love how the poster has love-hearts all over it," Sarah said.

If you were in the know, the Fun Love party poster design made it obvious that this party was going to be an ecstasy-fueled event and we were dying to be a part of it.

The next day, after school with a few weeks to go until the party, I changed into my 501 Levi Jeans, put on a tight white Bonds t-shirt, gelled my hair back, and laced up my black Doc Martin shoes, going from school uniform to dance party uniform. I smiled at my reflection in the mirror on my way out, pleased with what I saw.

I caught the 380 bus and met Anna across from Paddington Town Hall. She had walked up from where she and her Mum lived at Five Ways. Anna was wearing the same dance party uniform I was. The only difference in how we each looked was her long blond hair had been tied back in a ponytail with a red paisley bandana.

Anna smiled when she saw me get off the bus. "You look so good!"

"So do you!" I grinned at Anna. We kissed each other on the cheek, just like I used to with Tiffany. It felt like the right thing to do.

It was like we were a pair of models who'd stepped off the page of a Levi's advertisement onto Oxford Street. The early afternoon sun began to set as peak hour traffic sped past. We walked to Folkways Music store.

"I can't wait to go to this party!" I spoke with excitement.

"I hope they sell us tickets." Anna crossed her fingers.

Getting the tickets from Folkways Music store was easy. There were no hesitations or funny looks from the guy behind the counter. This time, the same man was pleasant and friendly. I think he recognised me from the last time.

"Have a great time! It's going to be a good event!"

With the tickets in our hands, we had passed the test. It was the passport that would lead us to try our first ecstasy pill and have one of the many most incredible moments of my young life.

SWEATBOX MELTDOWN

I TOOK MY SECOND ecstasy pill when we returned to the Hordern Pavilion for another massive dance party called Sweatbox Meltdown. It was also Evelyn's 17th birthday. To my friend's collective horror, Evelyn had invited Elizabeth along. This was so Evelyn would have someone else to hang with who wasn't going to take drugs. None of us could believe that Elizabeth had agreed to come, especially after all she's said about us going to dance parties.

Before going to the party, we met at Evelyn's place.

Evelyn lived with her dad and two brothers in a cramped two and a half-bedroom apartment. There wasn't much room for us to hang out while we waited for Evelyn to get ready.

"This place is so messy," Lee whispered to me as we sat on a stained couch.

"It's because Evelyn has no mum," Elizabeth whispered back, overhearing Lee.

Anna rolled her eyes. I knew exactly what she was thinking. Elizabeth had a way of being insensitive towards other people's feelings. I don't know how she'd ever gotten to be on the school council. I suspected the teachers had handpicked her because she was such a teacher's pet. Now here she was, about to go to her very first dance party with us. None of us wanted Elizabeth to come to the party.

When I'd heard Elizabeth was attending, I'd thought it was a joke. Our group had been full of objections:

"She'll totally ruin our fun!"

"Elizabeth is such a hypocrite if she comes along!"

"After all she said about us going to dance parties!"

"Isn't Elizabeth frightened she'll catch AIDS or something by hanging out with us?"

But Evelyn didn't seem to care how much we were against Elizabeth joining our group to go to the Hordern. So, we were stuck with her for the night.

As we waited for Evelyn to finish doing her hair and make-up, Lee asked Elizabeth what had happened to Evelyn's mum, "Does she still live in Tonga?"

"She passed away when Evelyn was nine years old," Elizabeth lowered her voice. "Don't tell anyone, but there were rumours her mum committed suicide. I remember they were saying it happened because she suffered with depression."

Anna bit her lower lip uncomfortably and Lee gave me a pained look.

We hadn't even got to the party and Elizabeth was already being a massive downer. I felt bad for Evelyn. I couldn't imagine what it would be like turning seventeen and not have my mum around to buy presents. I didn't know if what Elizabeth had said was true or made up. But I had the feeling there had to be some truth to it.

When Evelyn came out of her bedroom all dressed up, we cheered, "Happy Birthday!"

I noticed that as Evelyn entered the living room, her brothers acted like she wasn't even there. They were being weird and distant, pretending not to see Evelyn while they sat in the living room waiting for us to leave. It was hard to ignore Evelyn. She looked amazing in a tight, body-hugging, red mini-dress and had her hair teased up like a runway model.

We did the usual birthday stuff: lit seventeen candles on top of our favourite cake, Black Forrest, and sang Happy Birthday, out of tune. We gave presents such as a Prince's record, *Sign-o-the-times*. Prince was Evelyn's favourite singer. We took lots of photos and posed suggestively, cheering out, "Pose-mode!" as we proudly displayed our Sweat-box Meltdown tickets with excitement before we left for the Hordern.

As we waited for the 380 bus to come pick us up and take us to Paddington, I was so glad to get out of Evelyn's apartment. It reminded me how much worse-off some of my friends' home life was than mine. Suddenly, I couldn't understand why Evelyn refused to take drugs! If I lived like she did I would be the first one to get wasted. No wonder her brother was a stoner.

There were hundreds of party people waiting outside the gates of the Hordern Pavilion. Anna greeted some of the people she recognised from the Fun Love and Black parties, like Mini and Roger, and Fred, her riding instructor, and his partner. It felt like we belonged to an exclusive secret underground society.

"Who's that?" Elizabeth asked, suspicious.

"We met at the last party," Sarah explained with an air of superiority.

Elizabeth smiled back but looked jealous. To an outsider, it looked like we knew everyone at the party. Our group had extended friendships far beyond the school playground. As we received hugs and kisses from our new party people acquaintances, little did Elizabeth know we were on the hunt for drugs.

"Have you seen Steven?" I asked Michael.

"Not yet," Michael looked anxious. He knew exactly who I was looking for: Steven-the-Eckie-Man.

Evelyn grabbed my hand and led our group inside the Hordern Pavilion. The hall had been transformed into a futuristic, shiny industrial space. On each corner of the dance floor were functioning earth-moving excavators, ring-fenced with corrugated iron. Above the dance floor, mirror balls reflected lights onto the earth-moving equipment and green lasers shot pulsating beams across the bodies dancing with arms stretched towards the DJ booth elevated on a podium. DJ Tim Ritchie mixed a sample of Martin Luther King, Jr's groundbreaking speech, *I have a dream*, to a deep bass beat and the vocals of a no-name voice chanting, "Acid Man."

"This is the best birthday ever!" Evelyn smiled.

"What?" Elizabeth had to yell over the thunderous music. She was momentarily distracted at the sight of shirtless men dancing together. She couldn't take her eyes of the gay guys dressed like the Village People, wearing construction worker hard hats and tool belts. Many had already taken their shirts off, parading their perfect gym-toned chests as they stomped to the music in construction boots. "Looks more like a sex-show than a dance party!" Elizabeth laughed.

"I know!" Evelyn grinned. "Isn't it incredible?"

"Guys. We're just going to find someone," I announced, and took Anna's hand. Together, we pushed through the sweaty bodies, and we found Steven in the middle of the packed dance floor. He was wearing the same thing he'd worn at Fun Love: a singlet, bum bag, black cycle-shorts, and white volley tennis shoes. He looked so out of place compared to all the young, attractive people grooving around him. But that didn't stop us from being his 'friend.'

"Hi, Steven." I acted like we were best mates. "Got any eckies?"

"Sorry mate, sold out!" Steven kept dancing, completely off-his-face.

I felt utterly deflated and didn't know what to say. Upon seeing my disappointment, Steven grinned. "Follow me. I'll see if I can get some."

I took Steven's hand as he bounced through the dance floor on our mission of finding ecstasy. I wondered what people thought of us as they saw Anna and me with this strange middle-aged man wandering through the crowded dance floor. It must have been so obvious we were trying to score drugs. Or could it look like we were family? After all, Steven was old enough to be our father.

Anna tapped my shoulder. "People are following us!"

She wasn't being paranoid. Behind Anna was a conga line of the faces we'd met at Fun Love. Tonight, they were like Anna and I, *sober*, and hoping that Steven would show us where to find ecstasy.

Steven found a stocky young guy who was wearing a black nylon padded bomber jacket. On the back of the jacket were the words In Full Effect, embroidered in white. "How many do you want?" the young guy shouted.

"Five," I yelled back.

"One hundred dollars." The In Full Effect guy held out his hand. I handed over $100. The guy pulled out a plastic satchel full of white pills. There were at least thirty pills in there. He gave five to Steven, who handed them to me in full view of all the people dancing around us and cheering to the pounding music.

Anna and I grinned at each other, feeling so excited just at the sight of so many little white pills.

"Thank you so much!" Anna squeezed Steven's hand.

"Enjoy." He smiled, dancing on the spot as the giant stadium speakers boomed female vocals, *"Can you feel it?"*

This time the drug took effect faster and was much stronger. With giant smiles, we sang along to the music DJ Pee-Wee spun: Inner City's, *Good Life*. It was easy to sing along to, even when you were out-of-it, because the lyrics were so repetitive. You just had to sing the song title over and over. On ecstasy, this was the best song ever. *Good life* was such an instant crowd-pleaser that suddenly there was hardly any room left to dance. Above our heads, an excavator bucket swung into motion as we got squashed against a mass of bodies dripping with sweat. Hands were stretched towards the lights and the metal buckets of the excavators as they moved up and down. On ecstasy, it looked like the industrial excavators had come to life and were dancing with the party people.

Each breath felt like I was astral travelling across the dance floor. I noticed that Evelyn and Elizabeth weren't smiling. I felt embarrassed for them. They must have been the only ones in the massive crowd of six thousand people who hadn't taken ecstasy! Suddenly, I felt it was my mission to lighten Evelyn and Elizabeth's mood.

"I'm so glad you're here!" I told Elizabeth.

She smiled back but didn't look like she was enjoying herself.

"Are you having a good time?" I yelled with a giant grin and bulging eyes.

Elizabeth gave Evelyn an uncomfortable glance. She couldn't handle seeing a school friend acting so high on drugs, dancing so fast, and sweating profusely. It didn't help that I had an uncontrollable urge to prove everything was fine.

"You should come out with us all the time!" I kept going on and on, having no idea what I was saying. I thought I was telling Elizabeth how good I felt that she was at a dance party with us, but my words got muddled. A jumble of messages rolled out. Before I knew it, I confessed something to Elizabeth that was false.

"I truly love you, Elizabeth. Always have done. That's why I'm so glad you're here!"

Elizabeth stopped dancing and stared at me in shock.

"Really?" She placed her hand over her heart. "I had no idea you felt this way! Is that why you pretend not to like me at school?"

I was in another world and took Elizabeth into my arms and pressed my body against hers in a loving, eckie hug. This confirmed to Elizabeth that what I'd just told her was true. Actions speak louder than words. "I love this song!" I released Elizabeth and began to dance wildly. In my elated mind, I fully believed all I'd done was simply tell Elizabeth that I was glad she was here and hoped she was having a great time.

Meanwhile, Elizabeth stood frozen in the position I had just hugged her in, trying to process the idea that I loved her and always had done so. "Honestly, I had no idea you felt this way!" Elizabeth grabbed my arm. "I'm flattered and need some time to think about how this makes me feel."

As Elizabeth spoke, her words chipped away at my chemically fueled view of the world. An inner voice reminded me of one minor detail: *aren't I gay?* Had I lost my mind? Did I just confess to secretly being in love with a girl I didn't even like that much to begin with? I came back to reality and realised that I hadn't even wanted Elizabeth to come along tonight because she was so anti-drugs and homophobic. What I'd said to Elizabeth was a million miles from the truth! Was I hiding the truth so hard it was manifesting itself in scary new ways? Or was it the ecstasy turning me into something I wasn't? Either way,

I felt too happy to care. So, I kept dancing. The music was so perfect. Nothing else mattered. I was on E and in my own perfect little world.

Ecstasy made everyone at the Hordern uncontrollably chatty and cuddly with complete strangers. We said heaps of things we didn't mean. But at the time, no one cared because we truly believed that what we'd said was one hundred percent real. Ecstasy intensified every emotion and made us believe that everything we felt was real, so that if you *liked* someone you would really believe that you *loved* them.

Ecstasy was making all of us do things we'd never normally do in real life, like get along with one another, loving one another's company, and feeling good about being together in the same place. There were no fights breaking out, despite all the different types of people being under the same roof. There was no tension or aggression. Rather, there was an overwhelming feeling of everyone being loved and loving being part of the mass of bodies dancing to the house music.

In desperate need of water at the bar area, Sarah introduced me to a girl named Elle who went to an exclusive private school. Elle looked like she was around our age. But in the dark, and on drugs, who could tell?

"What are you on?" I asked.

"Nothing, darling!" Elle squealed with enormous, black, dilated pupils. Elle introduced us to her group of friends. One of them, Roger, had a little brown bottle pressed up to his nostril.

"What's that?" Anna asked.

"Rush," Roger explained.

"Rush?" Anna asked having no clue.

"Amyl nitrate." Roger handed Anna the bottle. "Have a sniff. It will blow you away!"

Since we'd taken ecstasy and nothing bad had happened, Anna was ready to try anything. She took Roger's advice and nearly fell over when the vapor hit her brain. I had to help Anna stand up and not lose balance.

"Are you ok?" I laughed.

"Yes! That was wild." Anna passed the little brown bottle to me and began to dance like a maniac screaming, "Woo hoo!"

I took a sniff from the little brown bottle. It smelt like chlorine or some heavy-duty cleaning product. I passed the bottle on to Lee and Sarah just as everything started to feel larger...louder...brighter. I was having a pulsating out-of-body experience. The colours, music, lights, and people smiling around me became a kaleidoscope in my head. The sensation only lasted for a minute before I was back to normal. Well, as normal as one could feel high on ecstasy at The Hordern.

"Let's go tell everyone what we think of them!" Elle laughed and dragged us back to the dance floor.

"I love how ecstasy just makes you go along with idiotic suggestions." I grinned enthusiastically as we stumbled after Elle. The first target Elle and Roger commented on, or as they saw it tried to *help*, was a woman wearing a very unfashionable early-80s-style red leather dress.

"Lose the dress, honey!" Elle waved her hand.

The woman looked insulted as she stared back at Elle. "Do I know you?" she asked.

I began to laugh, thinking the woman had hair like Princess Diana. "Who invited the royalty?" I giggled.

"Yeah, love, we're just here to help." Roger grinned as we moved through the crowd.

Ecstasy suddenly made us a very opinionated group of sixteen-year-olds.

"Hey, what's the hold up?" Elle yelled at a group of people blocking our path.

Anna grabbed my hand and slapped my palm across the backside of a woman standing in front of us.

The woman spun around and looked surprised. She looked like she was expecting to see a familiar face and then got confused because she didn't recognise us.

Anna and I gasped because it wasn't a woman's bum we'd slapped at all, but a seven-foot-tall drag queen.

"Well, hello gorgeous." The drag queen sparkled in a silver sequin dress. She had enormous fake breasts and wore a towering blond wig. Her lipstick and eyebrows were exaggerated, and she wore thick foundation cream covering her Adam's apple.

"You are gorgeous!" Anna exclaimed.

The drag queen spoke with a deep, manly voice, "Thanks sweetheart. So are you, dear."

As we wandered through the endless parade of people dancing in a trance, Anna yelled in my ear, "This is what makes the Hordern such a special place. It's not just the music or dancing — it's because of the perfect mix of people."

"And the ecstasy!" I reminded Anna.

"It's not just the ecstasy." Anna couldn't stop talking, "It totally doesn't matter who or what you are here! You can be gay or straight or cross-gender, black or white. It just doesn't matter — everyone belongs."

"Yeah, because of the ecstasy!"

"In real life, none of these people would be so open and friendly."

"I know! If you passed these people on the street during the day they wouldn't even give you a second glance. Let alone a smile. Here, you get kisses and hugs!"

The next morning, I shared a taxi home with Anna and Sarah. We talked about how Elizabeth and Evelyn hadn't looked like they'd had a good time.

"I think it's kind of selfish the way they acted." Sarah twirled a lock of her red hair.

"I know," Anna agreed, "They were acting like we shouldn't have had as much fun as we did."

"Like it was a bad thing to have a good time," I added.

"They had every chance to have just as good a time as we did," Anna noted.

"I wonder what upset them so much?" I said, completely clueless and brain-dead the morning after.

"They're simply scared to do what we do," Sarah replied.

"From the looks on their faces, it was like they expected us to hold their hands through the whole experience," Anna said. "It was like they needed us to be their babysitter or something."

"Yeah, drug babysitters!" I giggled.

We didn't care what the taxi driver could overhear.

Monday morning, and no longer under the influence of ecstasy, none of us felt like getting off the school bus when it stopped outside Dover Heights High. By the end of rollcall, practically every student in year 11 knew what our group had gotten up to on the weekend. Evelyn showed the photos that had been taken at her place before we had gone to the party. The students standing beside Evelyn saw what we were wearing, how we were posing with our arms all over each other, holding our dance party tickets with pride and grinning from ear to ear.

"So, what goes on at these parties?" Sonia asked.

"Everyone just dances till sunrise," Evelyn answered.

The admiration continued from a group of girls:

"Cool."

"How did you get in?"

"Aren't you meant to be over eighteen?"

Evelyn relished the attention, knowing that many kids in school were jealous they hadn't been invited to her birthday party, or gone to The Hordern.

That's when we officially became known as The Group.

DRUG BUST

A S AUTUMN APPROACHED, school and homework took up more and more time. We had no choice but to miss out on the dance parties being held every second weekend at the Hordern Pavilion. With just a year and a half to go until we sat for the HSC, none of us wanted to stuff up any more qualifying exams. When we talked about what we hoped to be when we grew up, we came to the same conclusion: "To make it, you had to get good score in the HSC." And to do that would mean going to fewer dance parties.

As it turned out, Sweatbox Meltdown was the last dance party Evelyn would ever go to with The Group. After the party, Elizabeth convinced Evelyn that we were no longer the right friends to hang out with and she stopped talking to us in class. Just like that. Like we were strangers and not best friends. But what hurt most was that Evelyn didn't even say goodbye before she changed schools a few weeks later.

Her Dad moved Evelyn and her brothers to the Western suburbs, to live in a bigger home than the tiny apartment they had rented in Dover Heights. This was how our friendship with Evelyn ended.

A few weeks later, riding on the school bus home, Sarah pointed out the window. There was a billboard poster sticky taped to the light post. It read, April Fool Fun. It was being held at the Hordern Pavilion on the 1st of April.

"There's going to be another Fun party!" Anna became as excited as if she was on ecstasy. If it had been any other party we would have given it the flick. But because it was a Fun party, we just couldn't resist.

"We have to go!" I was super excited.

"Fuck the HSC!" Sarah smiled.

On the weekend, we bought tickets from Disco City Records in the city, on Pitt Street. Behind the counter there was a shelf with DJ merchandise plus a row of twenty little brown bottles of Rush. They were selling amyl nitrate!

"Can we also have one of those?" I asked the guy behind the counter casually. Just like my first-time buying booze, the guy behind the counter said nothing as he popped the tiny brown bottle into a tiny brown paper bag. The sales assistant acted like it wasn't a big deal.

The week before the April Fool Fun party, I caught a news story on TV as I read my economics textbook. In Sydney there had been a huge ecstasy pill drug bust by the Australian Federal Police. It had been the first ever major haul of its kind by authorities. The street value of the seizure was over one million dollars.

I phoned Anna instantly. "Are you watching TV?"

"No. Why?"

"Turn on the ABC news."

Anna and I watched the end of the story together over the phone, watching footage of the police carrying giant plastic bags filled with thousands of chunky white pills.

"That's so unfair." Anna sounded indignant, adding, "How rude of them to do that right before a major dance party."

"I know!"

Anna said, "It's probably going to be so much harder to score ecstasy now."

When the news story had come on I had been studying Adam Smith's theory of the invisible hand, which he used to explain how those who seek wealth by following their individual self-interest also assist society as a whole and build the common good in *The Wealth of Nations*. We had all laughed at this in class, saying, *"Watch out here comes the invisible hand."* But sitting in front of the TV, watching the news, the coin dropped — I finally got how, in a free competitive market, goods and services perceived as most beneficial or of the highest quality are the most profitable.

It explained the street value of ecstasy.

This lesson in supply and demand truly affected me. But I doubted I could use this example in my HSC exam. "We'll have to be on the lookout for dud pills." I sighed. "I hate how the news makes out what the police have done is such a good thing; like they're doing it for the community."

Anna said, "All they've done is just spoiled our fun."

"It will totally ruin the Fun party if we can't get any Es!"

Even at sixteen years old, the thought of us going to a dance party without being on ecstasy was now incomprehensible. It would be like leaving the house without brushing your teeth or wearing clean underwear.

"I wish it was legalised," Anna urged.

"Me, too. It's so much better than alcohol," I agreed.

APRIL FOOL FUN

"EVERYONE'S WAITING FOR Steven-the-Eckie-Man." Lee cocked his head towards the familiar faces of party people waiting beyond the gates at the Hordern Pavilion. They stood with folded arms and teeth chattering in the cold night air. None looked as happy as usual. It was obvious they weren't just waiting for friends to arrive.

"Hey, check them out." Anna's eyes gazed at two middle-aged men in very plain clothes.

"They look like they've shopped at Best & Less!" Sarah laughed.

But it was no joke. Both men looked very serious walking through the crowd. It was obvious they weren't party people; they were patrol people.

"Do you think they're undercover drug cops?" Simon asked.

"Shit — bet they are!" Lee looked a bit freaked out.

"It doesn't make sense how something so fun is so illegal." Anna shrugged.

Seeing the undercover cops brought home the reality that if we asked the wrong person for ecstasy, we could get into serious trouble. It was hard to believe that the most wonderful experience we'd ever had was against the law. At sixteen, none of us felt like we were engaging in criminal activity. We just wanted to have some fun.

"I feel paranoid having the bottle of Rush in my jeans pocket," I whispered. My friends laughed, but I wasn't joking.

Midnight came and our dealer Steven-the-Eckie-Man was nowhere to be seen. It was like he'd known not to turn up to this party. I hoped he didn't get busted. We hit the dance floor, but it didn't have the usual fun atmosphere of the Hordern Pavilion. It felt wrong dancing to house music without being high on E. Normally, by midnight the whole party would be grinning from ear to ear. But tonight, the crowd was unnervingly calm.

"Maybe we should ask some regulars if they know where to get some E?" Anna suggested.

"Good idea," I agreed. I spotted Michael with Sally on the dance floor and like us, they were not enjoying being sober.

"What a bad April fools' prank!" Michael joked.

"What do you mean?" I asked.

"Well, who ever heard of a dance party without any dealers or E?"

"Wait a minute." Michael's girlfriend Sally suddenly looked alert. "We've bought Es off him before." Sally pointed at a tall, Nordic looking man with a razor sharp blond flat top. He wore army camouflage print cargo pants. Sally introduced us; his name was Sven and we followed him towards the back stalls, away from the crowds.

"You're not with the police?" He looked me in the eye.

"No." I nearly laughed and handed over $100.

But Sven only handed back 2 pills.

"What's this?" I protested, "I paid you for five!"

"They are fifty each," Sven said in a thick European accent. "These Es are imported from Amsterdam."

What choice did we have? It was nearly 1am and we hadn't taken anything yet. It wasn't like there were any other dealers working the Hordern at this party. Without ecstasy the Fun party was no fun at all.

"We'll have to halve them," I told my friends.

"Ripped off!"

"I blame the police for this."

"Pigs!"

I bit the two ecstasy pills in half and ignored the vile acidic taste. That wasn't going to put me off having a good time.

An hour later, we were still waiting to feel elated. The Amsterdam ecstasy wasn't as strong as normal. The effect was totally diluted compared to what we had scored from Steven-the-Eckie-Man. Also, we'd only had half each. By 4 a.m., the ecstasy felt mildly pleasant. Not too strong, but nice and dreamy. I floated across the dance floor. Everything was covered with glitter as the DJ played Joe Smooth's, *Promised Land*. It was like we'd been transport back in time to a 1970s disco from another galaxy, a stadium sized version of Studio 54.

Anna and Sarah were dancing on the podium next to me and Lee. We looked at each other and smiled with pure contentment. On the next podium, Michael was dancing with Sally. I saw Michael wave at me, and I waved back. We both had the same blissed-out smile as the music boomed. We were at peace as we danced to the progressive house beat.

I had a sense of complete solidarity with the world, knowing that across the globe, from London to New York, there were people like us all sharing this same experience. It didn't matter that we were living in Sydney, Australia. For the first time, just for a moment, it felt like living in Australia wasn't being stuck on the other side of the world. That we weren't so isolated, but instead we were part of something bigger. We were part of something very important sweeping through the planet, changing people for the better, making us more open and happier.

Sarah interrupted my dance of contentment. She'd noticed some girls from our school across the dance floor. "Hey? Aren't they in the year below us?"

"No!" Anna said, "They're two grades below us!"

The girls from Dover Heights were in year 9. They were dressed as goths and looked like they were suffering from heat exhaustion from wearing long velvet dresses on the sweaty dance floor. Their deathly white face make-up and dark eye-mascara was running down their checks from the heat. It looked like it was their first time at a major dance party.

"It's weird seeing a bunch of fourteen-year-olds on the dance floor of the Hordern! Don't you think?" Sarah said.

"Everything with this party is so wrong tonight," Lee agreed.

The fourteen-year-olds weren't the most popular or loudest girls in their year at Dover, yet somehow tonight they looked like they belonged to the party people crowd, dressed in their goth outfits, wearing too much make-up.

"I can't believe they're here!" Anna shouted over the music. "They're so young, aren't they?"

"It's like every generation breaks into the adult world younger and younger these days," Sarah said.

On Tuesday morning, Anna told me about another encounter she'd had with the year 9 goth girls. It had happened just after the recess bell set off a slow march back to class. The goth girls had approached Anna in the girls' toilet, looking nervous and self-conscious.

Frieda, the group's ringleader, who also wore the most mascara out of her friends had said, "Great party on Saturday! Do you know where we can get us some eckie?"

Anna said, at first she had been startled to hear these words come out of a junior. Immediately Anna said she felt paranoid that someone would overhear them and told Frieda, "I don't sell drugs!"

The goth girls looked at Anna with surprise. "But you know where to get them right?"

Anna said she had to check that no one else was within earshot. Thankfully, all the other students were making their way back to class.

"We always get it at the dance party," Anna told them.

"Oh," the goth girls sounded disappointed. "Can you get us some next time?"

"I can't believe they asked you that!" I laughed when Anna told me, seated at the back of the 11A English class.

"They were so sincere and clueless," Anna whispered. "I'm still in disbelief that I've just been asked to score drugs in the high school toilet. It's so wrong being asked by a group of fourteen-year-old girls — who I barely know — if I could score ecstasy for them!"

"It's like something out of one of those tacky 70s anti-drug movies the teachers showed us in year eight."

"Yeah, instead of *Go Ask Alice*, it's *Go Ask Anna*."

On the face of it, we were the most unlikely kids in the entire school playground to score drugs from. We no longer smoked cigarettes or drank alcohol and didn't belong to any of the stoner groups that ditched classes or hung out at the bottom playground. We pulled good grades and were in the top 10% of our class. We weren't like the ones who'd dropped out of school before they reached the year 10 school certificate.

"It must have taken them a lot of guts to ask you that," I told Anna.

"I don't like that they think I'd just sell them drugs. Do you think we are getting a bad reputation?"

"Doubt it. It's just that they saw us at the Hordern. I don't think anyone else would suspect a thing."

Anna smiled. I knew the last thing she wanted was to be viewed as a druggie. Her biggest fear was that her mum might find out. "I would never be brave enough to ask a senior that when I was fourteen."

"Me neither!" I agreed. Since starting high school, I had become a victim of bullying and name-calling, but I had never been forced to take drugs in the boys' toilet like I had been warned could happen. It just hadn't been the case. Things were all backwards to how everyone thought it would be. Now that I was sixteen years old, a senior, it was the younger kids who wanted the older kids to supply them with drugs.

SWEATBOX 'LET THEM EAT CAKE'

"GUESS WHO?" TIFFANY'S voice boomed through the telephone line and she had the best news. "I've moved back to Australia!!"

"Why didn't you tell me?" I couldn't believe she was back.

"I wanted it to be a surprise! Ha ha," Tiffany chuckled over the phone, and I realised how much I'd missed her laugh. "Mum and John, my stepdad, relocated to Sydney — so here I am!" Over the phone we caught up about what we'd been doing lately.

I told Tiffany about dance parties and taking ecstasy with Anna and The Group.

"Anna at a dance party?" Tiffany exclaimed. "No way, man! Shut up! You're shittin' me right?" Tiffany had developed a heavy American accent in a very short time. Which I immediately thought was a bad sign.

"For real!" I laughed. "We're totally into house music and ecstasy."

"I don't get what this *house* music stuff is all about. The cool kids in the States, like in Santa Monica, were into dropping acid! Oh my God, Nathan! Have you ever gone tripping?"

I didn't know what *tripping* was.

"No."

"You must try acid! It's totally out of control!"

"Isn't acid a 60s hippy drug?"

"No way, man! It's wild! You see all these colours and traces of things! It's wicked!"

This proved to me how house music was more of a London movement than an American one. I suddenly got scared thinking about what sort of person the United States had turned Tiffany into. Our group hated American fashion, compared to European. Tacky American is how we described tragic US pop stars like Debbie Gibson with her bubble-gum pop, like *Electric Youth*. It was such formulaic commercial crap compared to the underground house music movement.

"What about cocaine?" Tiffany asked.

"What about it?" I asked nonchalantly.

"Have you tried it?" Tiffany asked over-excited.

"No," I answered obliviously.

"Really? Everyone in the States does it. I did a line at school one morning and finally algebra made sense!" Tiffany giggled. "So, when are we going to meet up?"

We arranged to meet at Bondi Junction the next day after school. When I stepped off the school bus and laid eyes on Tiffany for the first time in over a year, we both screamed. Tiffany grabbed me and we jumped ecstatically in a circle. "I can't believe how good you look!"

"Me too!" I felt almost as happy as I did when I popped an E. "I love your hair!" Tiffany had shaved her hair off on the right-side and the other side was dyed bright red and teased out. She wore black leather boots, a pink mini-skirt, and a black leather biker jacket over a loose fitted t-shirt with a print of The Cure's *Kiss me, Kiss me, Kiss me,* album cover. She was totally punk now. I felt so daggy dressed in my school uniform and backpack.

We caught up on each other's lives over two servings of large french fries at McDonald's. Tiffany couldn't stop talking about how cool the kids in America were compared to Australia. I started to find it annoying but didn't say anything.

"You'd like it in the States. They have these massive parties on Venice Beach where everyone drops acid and dances around giant bonfires. The fire makes you hallucinate. It's mental!"

I told Tiffany all about our ecstasy experiences. "The scene here has completely changed since we went to The Exchange. The Hordern Pavilion is like The Exchange times ten! I can't wait for you to come to a dance party with us! You're not going to believe the scale of it."

"Man, I can't wait to go tripping with you!" Tiffany ate the last french fry. We didn't care how loud we spoke or that everyone else within the family restaurant could overhear us. It made talking about drugs even more fun.

The next day, Anna and I picked up tickets to another Sweatbox party after school; it was called Let Them Eat Cake.

Tiffany visited us at Dover Heights High at the end of the week during lunch period. "Man, this place hasn't changed a bit!" She sounded unimpressed. Everyone in the school playground stopped and stared, including the teachers. Tiffany wasn't wearing a school uniform, dressed instead in Doc Martin boots, black tights, a mini-skirt, and her leather jacket.

I gave Tiffany her dance party ticket.

"Cool," Tiffany smiled. "What about the E?"

"We'll get them at the Hordern."

The next time I saw Tiffany was at the party.

"So, this is it?" Tiffany sounded impressed as we stood outside the entrance to the Hordern in the freezing night air. Hundreds of excited party people headed into the stately pavilion, and we followed. There was only one person we wanted to see.

The interior of the Hordern Pavilion had been transformed into a stately ball room. There were Roman columns on each end of the dance floor, silk curtains and a giant mirror ball reflecting light over the people. Some who took the party's theme literally, and dressed in outfits of aristocrats from the French Revolution period.

Anna cheered when she spotted Steven-the-Eckie-Man among the aristocrats. "He's back!"

Tiffany's jaw dropped as she watched Anna walk up to Steven to score drugs. She remembered how Anna had used to look down on us when we went on drinking binges. Now Anna was scoring ecstasy for her mates at a dance party. Things had changed in the time that Tiffany had been away.

Even in the middle of winter, Steven wore his same bicycle shorts, bum-bag, and Dunlop volley sandshoes with a yellow smiley face t-shirt. One of the side-effects of ecstasy is that it raises body temperature, so you don't feel the cold. That's why there were always so many half-naked people dancing all night high on ecstasy.

"Enjoy!" Anna brought back seven white speckled pills in the palm of her hand, "Tiffany, you're going to love this. They're called American Party Ecstasy!"

"Funny, how you had to come back to Australia to try it," Lee teased.

We got a drink and swallowed the pills without hesitation and hit the dance floor. The light-headed effect came on faster than usual and Anna grabbed my arm. "I've got to go for a walk!"

This ecstasy felt different to all the other ones we'd taken previously. It came on very lightly. Then suddenly it engulfed my entire body with such force it was like a bomb had gone off, like someone had flicked a switch that made every limb and organ in my body blissfully numb. The only expression I could muster was a big smile. Suddenly, I had no idea where I was, or who I was, as we wandered through an endless stream of smiling happy party people. From the expressions on the faces around us it was obvious they were feeling the same sensation.

Anna couldn't stop smiling either as we held onto each other. Somehow, we lost Tiffany in the crowd along with Lee, Sarah, and Simon.

"It's so strong!" I could barely stand up.

"This is the best ecstasy ever!" Anna let out a huge breath and inhaled deeply. We didn't feel the cold winter night air at all as we walked with our arms around each other like a couple in love. Blissfully happy and having the deepest conversation of our lives. "I feel so connected to you," Anna admitted.

"I've never connected with anyone like this in my life before," I agreed.

"Me too!" Anna almost yelled.

"I feel like, I could tell you anything and it wouldn't matter." I felt incredibly close to Anna, emotionally, mentally, and physically. I'd thought I could only feel this way about a man: Campbell. But tonight, it felt different. All my life, Tiffany had been my number one girlfriend. But since Tiffany had gone away to America and I'd discovered dance parties and ecstasy with Anna, everything had changed. My feelings towards Anna had grown a thousand times stronger.

As if reading my mind, Anna told me, "I'm so glad we are such good friends. I feel so lucky to know you. I hope we stay friends for the rest of our lives!"

"I know! We're so similar, I really feel like I can be myself when I'm with you." I wanted to tell Anna I was gay but instead said, "We're a special kind of people." Even though I'd lost all my inhibitions, and was surrounded by thousands of same sex couples, I still couldn't reveal or face the truth.

We held onto each other as the warm, loving sensation of MDMA circulated through our veins. The serotonin level in our brain was elevated like never before, rendering us both powerless to do anything but to confess repeatedly how much we loved each other. That's when the marriage proposal came up. Not from me but from Anna. Or was it the ecstasy talking?

"We should get married!" Anna hinted.

"Yes!" I agreed enthusiastically as we looked deeply into each other's dilated pupils. Unlike most marriage proposals, ours wasn't sealed with a kiss. We un-wrapped a stick of chewing gum and tore it in half.

"These Es are so strong!" Anna let out a deep breath.

I held Anna close and promised myself I'd never tell anyone I was gay. Suddenly, I realised getting married would be the perfect cover. "We'll make a great couple!" I grinned. Then it hit me – what about my other great love? "We better find Tiffany," I said with some concern.

"Yeah…she won't…be used to this!" Anna could barely speak.

The Hordern Pavilion was dark and filled to capacity with thousands of people dancing wildly.

My vision was blurred. It was impossible to find Tiffany or any of our other friends. All around us it seemed like every person had taken a pill from the same batch. The same exuberant expression was written on every face. People were smiling at complete strangers, with a common unspoken knowledge: *You are on E. And it is the best thing in the world!* All the beautiful people were dancing with beautiful strangers. No one was snubbing anyone. The drugs made sure of that.

"There she is!" Anna spotted Tiffany dancing with a tall guy who had a ten-inch spiky mohawk. We ran to Tiffany. Tiffany grabbed hold of us and started to laugh hysterically. There were no words to express what we were feeling or thinking. We laughed non-stop for ten minutes before anyone one could speak.

"How good does this feel?" I screamed.

"Why didn't you tell me?" Tiffany laughed.

"I tried to!" I laughed. "Is it better than acid?"

"Way better!" Tiffany exclaimed.

"Who's this?" Anna asked regarding the shirtless young man holding Tiffany's waist.

"Meet my new best friend, Dave," Tiffany introduced the punk boy. Dave wore Doc Martin boots, torn jeans, and no shirt. His chest was tanned, and he had a pierced nipple.

"You kids are shitfaced!" Dave looked amused.

"Kids? How old do you think I am?" Tiffany asked.

"I don't know. Twenty?" Dave shrugged.

"Twenty!" Tiffany laughed. "No way man. I'm sixteen."

"Shit! You're just babies!" Dave laughed.

"How old are you?" I asked Dave.

"Nineteen. What about you? Are you also sixteen?"

I nodded and looked at Anna and Tiffany. "It's so much fun to spin people out about how old we really are!"

"In the dark and on drugs — who can tell how old anyone is?" A stylish girl dancing next to Dave grinned at me. "You don't look sixteen!"

"Thanks. How old are you?" I asked.

"Seventeen." She smiled and took my hand. "I'm Belinda. What's your name?"

"Nathan." Before I realised what was going on, Belinda was kissing me on the lips, her arms were around me and her tongue was in my mouth. Green lasers shot beams around our silhouette as we embraced. I was so wasted I didn't know what I was doing, or who I was doing it with. "What are you on?" I asked.

"Ecstasy, acid, and speed." Belinda's eyes rolled as she said, "Sixteen is such a sexy age. Next time, you must come out with me and my friends!"

"Okay!" I agreed, wide-eyed, and we swapped phone numbers.

We had sweated so much it was like we'd had a shower fully dressed. I was soaked. There was nothing else to say or do except dance. We moved to the tremendous sound of house music along with thousands of others. Bottles of water, chewing gum, and Chupa Chups lollipops were being passed around. At 4 a.m., the music grew more intense, with fewer vocals, more bass, and electronically altered voices. Sweat dripped from our foreheads, our eyes were wide, and a bright light shined in our faces from an SBS TV film crew wandering through the dance floor. They were filming what was going on. They filmed Tiffany dancing with Dave. Tiffany waved at the camera. Then Anna, Lee, Sarah, and I did the same with big ecstasy grins.

We were famous for fifteen seconds.

PROFESSIONAL PARTY BOYS

THE FOLLOWING MONDAY night, I received a phone call from Belinda. We spoke for an hour about everything, from how long we've been taking ecstasy, to how Belinda also lived at home with her parents. She lived in Hurstville with her older brother, Brad. He was twenty-one, studying medicine at Sydney University, and he was openly gay. I liked that it didn't matter to Belinda that her brother was gay. She didn't sound ashamed, but rather proud.

She was more worried about her exams. "I'm meant to be preparing for my HSC. I'm in year 12. Can't believe exams are less than three months away now! I'm finding it so hard to study lately." We talked about other drugs like acid, speed, and cocaine. Belinda revealed that one of her school friends had tried heroin. "She had the worst experience on it. She said she felt like she was going to die."

"Really?"

"It made her vomit, but after telling me this she said she'd probably do it again!"

"Can't believe she'd want to take it again. It sounds gross."

"I know! There's no way you'd catch me doing heroin!"

"Me neither! Never ever!"

"Why would you do a drug if it turns you into a zombie?"

"Heroin is a drug for people who are of a lower class," I said in a hushed voice.

"Oh. Totally. My friend who took heroin would never go to a dance party. She only goes to see live bands!"

"How boring."

She said, "Heroin is so passé." Then she asked, "Are you going to the next dance party?"

"For sure!"

"Would you like to come with us?"

"Sure!" I agreed. I hoped my friends wouldn't mind.

But it wasn't an issue. At school, no one was interested in going to the next party.

"I say we give it a miss." Lee shrugged.

"Yeah, I can't really afford it." Sarah agreed.

"Let's wait for a really good one," Anna said. "It's like there's one every week now."

She was right. The free street press, 3-D Magazine, joked that it was Club Hordern now, because there was a dance party held there practically every Saturday night. So, I decided to go with my newfound friend.

This is how I returned to The Exchange for the first time since I had been fifteen-years-old. But this time, I wasn't there to pick up. I was there to meet Belinda and her brother, Brad. Everything inside The Exchange was the same as I remembered: wall-to-wall men in light blue jeans and tight t-shirts, checking each other out. For the first time in ages, I really thought about Campbell and wondered why he hadn't called since that last drunken phone call at 3am. I missed him.

I was relieved to see Belinda and Brad arrive.

Brad went to the mirror bar and scored trips from a dealer, then drove us to the Hordern in a red Jeep that his parents had bought for him for his 21st birthday.

I felt so adult hanging out with these new friends. I was so proud of myself that I'd made such cool friends who didn't even go to my school! Until Brad asked me the one question I wasn't ready for. "Are you gay, bi, or straight?"

"Straight!" I was caught off guard by how blatantly Brad had asked this. My cheeks flushed.

"Really?" Brad's eyes met mine through the rear vision mirror. "I was surprised when I saw my little sister pashing you on the dance floor last week. I'm sure I'd seen you out before."

"No. No, I'm straight! Just into the dance party scene, that's all."

My heart pounded as I wondered, *could Belinda's gay brother Brad tell I was secretly gay? Had he seen me out before, with Campbell?*

"Don't get me wrong." Brad smiled. "It's a compliment for a gay guy to think a straight guy is gay. It means you've got a good sense of style."

I wondered if it was time to tell the truth. But fear gripped me. *What if they told my school friends at the next dance party?*

"I'm cool with hanging out on the gay scene. My first girlfriend, Tiffany, took me to The Exchange when we were fifteen. You guys have the best parties!"

"They sure do!" Belinda grinned as we pulled into the car park.

It was freezing outside, our breath turned to mist as we shivered.

Brad opened a plastic satchel that contained three small squares of coloured paper. I watched Belinda and Brad place the paper on their tongue. I held the small square paper on the tip of my index finger, unsure what to do next.

"You have to suck on it," Belinda explained.

Once it was in my mouth, I couldn't taste anything. Acid didn't have the vile taste of ecstasy. I chewed the tasteless paper and swallowed it, not expecting anything major to happen.

"It depends on your mood and the company you're in whether you have a good trip or not." Belinda held my hand reassuringly.

By midnight, I was moving with more energy than ever before. I was dancing with lightning speed, while my vision played tricks on me. Everything was distorted. As I looked at the crowd, coloured shapes bounced off the people on the floor and their faces started to look like people from TV. I checked my watch and could barely read the time. I danced with Belinda and Brad for nearly two hours without a break. I was having such a good time, but I didn't know if it was because I was with Belinda, or if it was the drugs or the party.

As I danced, an attractive shirtless man gave me the eye and I couldn't take my eyes off his naked chest until Belinda grabbed hold of me and spun me to face her. She gave me a surprised look. In that instant, I could tell she knew her brother had been right about me. But it was ok. Belinda didn't judge me, she just smiled and mouthed the words to the song the DJ was playing: Cappella's *Helyom Halib,* inviting us to work it.

I danced with Belinda, but I was in a world of my own, thinking about all the times I'd resisted looking back at guys who gave me longing looks. When I was with The Group, it was easier to ignore. I never gave in to my urges or responded to their advances, no matter how loving I felt on the love drug. But tonight, I wasn't with my school friends. I was with real party people, and they didn't care if I was gay or not.

At 5 a.m., I was dancing with Brad in front of the speakers while Belinda went to buy a bottle of water. From the corner of my eye, I saw the dance party's *"body boys,"* as Anna named them. I wasn't hallucinating; one of the body boys was watching me dance. I felt paranoid and pretended not to notice. Then I felt sweaty hands grab my waist and expected it to be Belinda. But it wasn't. It was one of the most handsome men from the body boys, smiling into my eyes and chewing gum with a big grin.

He was one of the hottest guys at a party with over six thousand hot guys, and he was making a move on me. He pressed his hard body up against mine and kissed me on the lips. It felt much better than my kiss with Belinda had last week. Time stopped for a second until my mind went into overdrive, thinking about who might just have seen what happened. What if the year 9 goth girls or Michael and Sally were somewhere in the crowd? I imagined how fast the gossip would travel! *Guess who was kissing a muscle queen at the Hordern?* What would it be like if news got out at school that someone saw me kissing a guy?

I pushed him away and ran for it.

Belinda and Brad found me near the exit.

"Are you ok?" Belinda asked.

I couldn't talk. I was freaking out.

Belinda rubbed my back. "It's okay. You're not ready."

I didn't say anything. I was so embarrassed. I was too far gone, and my heart was beating like crazy.

"You'll know when the time is right." Belinda gave me a warm hug.

"Please don't tell anyone," I pleaded terrified, thinking my life was going to be over as soon as the sun came up.

"Promise." Belinda and Brad both smiled. All I could see were psychedelic patterns swirling across their faces.

"You're going to be fine," Brad tried to reassure me. "I'm glad you didn't go too far with that guy."

"Yeah, he's a sleaze," Belinda agreed.

"You mean a rent boy," Brad said.

"What?" I was confused and weary.

"A prostitute," Brad explained. "He's a professional party boy. You don't want to get mixed up with that."

Brad and Belinda dropped me home just before 7 a.m. on Sunday morning.

Before I got out of Brad's Jeep, Belinda asked me if I had a good time.

"Yeah," I said, feeling wired and twitchy.

"What do your parents say when you come in at this hour?" Brad was curious.

"Not much." I shrugged. "They're just glad I come home, I guess. I broke them in at a young age."

"Do they know you take drugs?" Belinda asked.

"No." I smiled.

"Neither do ours." Belinda giggled. "Ours think we dance all night without any assistance."

We all chuckled at the thought until Brad said, "They probably do know, just don't want to admit it."

When I opened the front door, I found Mum doing the laundry

in her nightgown. Suddenly, I realised how off my face I still was. The walls shimmered like crushed velvet and all I could hear was high-pitched ringing. It was impossible to hear her over the sound of the washing machine.

"What?" I called out.

"I said you should give me your dirty clothes now to be washed! They stink of smoke!"

I stripped down to my underwear and gave Mum my smelly dance party clothes in the hallway. The sound from the washing machine was like a drum machine and house music began to play in my head.

Mum gave me a strange look as she watched me groove to the rhythm of the spin-cycle in my y-fronts.

I bobbed along to the mechanical rhythm and in my mind heard sounds from the Hordern, telling me to work it to the bone.

She said, "I don't know how you can still be in the mood to dance after being out all night."

"Huh?"

"I don't know how you can still be dancing!"

This made me giggle. Was she really that unaware?

But, unless you'd tried drugs for yourself, how would you know? Both my parents were the kind of people who simply didn't do that sort of thing. Even though they'd lived through the swinging 60s and the glitter years of the 70s, they'd never associated with people who took drugs. They weren't part of the counterculture. So, how could they now pick up on the tell-tale signs of their teenage son indulging in illegal substances, such as my dilated pupils, the constant chewing the morning after and now random dancing to the rhythm of white goods?

In a way, I wished my parents did know how good it was to take drugs and that it was ok. I wished that they would try ecstasy or acid. If they did, then maybe they'd stop fighting about money and stuff and get along with each other. Plus, they'd be fine with me doing it and I wouldn't have to hide a thing. We could all just get along and be one happy family for a change.

I headed straight for the shower and washed a night's worth of sweat off my body. As I closed my eyes, I could still see all the people in the Hordern dancing in my mind. My mind had been completely re-wired. Coming down from an acid trip, the party just lived on in my brain. It was almost impossible to fall asleep even though I was exhausted.

I just lied in my single bed, twitching, wide-eyed and feeling frustrated.

GO MENTAL ON ACID

AFTER EVELYN CHANGED schools, none of us heard from her for months. It was like she had disappeared off the face of the Earth, or had just completely forgotten about us. For a long time, what was left of our group talked about how weird it was that Evelyn had just left Dover without saying goodbye; it was like we hadn't been close friends after all. But that was nothing compared to how weird it was when I finally did hear from Evelyn again.

It was Thursday morning at 6:30 a.m. I was asleep when the phone rang.

My mum woke me up. "It's for you!" She handed me the portable phone. Mum was getting ready to leave for work. She gave me a stern look that emphasised how strange it was for me to get a phone call so early.

A shot of adrenaline rushed through my veins, thinking it would be Campbell. "Hello?" I answered with excitement.

"Nathan! Oh my god!" It took me a moment to place the voice and realise it was Evelyn. It sounded like she was calling from a public phone box and was yelling over the sound of street traffic. She also sounded like she was totally out-of-it. "I'm totally freaked out!"

I was confused. Evelyn had never taken drugs with us. She had always been so anti-drugs. I got excited at the thought that this may have changed since she'd moved to the Western suburbs. Why else would she be calling so early in the morning? She must have been out on a Wednesday night. Partying on a school night. *Cool,* I thought. "Evelyn?" I lowered my voice, "Are you tripping?"

"Tripping? No way! I wouldn't do drugs! Ever!"

At first, I didn't believe Evelyn because she sounded completely intoxicated. "Evelyn, why are you calling so early? I haven't heard from you in ages. What's up?"

"They're trying to get to me! I've been out all night running from them! They wouldn't allow me into any of the clubs in Kings Cross! How shameful! They looked at me and went, 'No way!'"

I started to worry as I listened to Evelyn rant so hysterically. I knew something was seriously wrong. I was sure Evelyn was on more than just acid. I'd never heard her, or anyone else, sound like this in my life. "Evelyn, seriously are you all right?"

"You have to help me! They're coming to get me!"

"What? Who??"

"They're trying to lock me up! Nathan, can I stay with you? Please!"

"Who's trying to get you Evelyn?"

"Oh no! Here they come! I've got to go!"

BEEP. BEEP. BEEP. Evelyn had hung up, leaving me with a disconnect tone and feeling unsettled and not knowing what to do as I got ready for school.

I told the rest of the group about the phone call as we waited for the school bus. No one believed me how weird Evelyn had sounded. But they did think it was weird that Evelyn had phoned out of the blue so early in the morning.

The next day, Elizabeth found out what was going on. She'd phoned Evelyn's home and learned that Evelyn hadn't been well. "Since they moved to Blacktown, the girls at Evelyn's new school have been such bitches. They pulled her hair and called her racist names. Evelyn dropped out of school a month ago," Elizabeth told us at recess. "Things got worse after that. One night, Evelyn woke up the entire house at 3 a.m., screaming that she'd made them breakfast. She fried two whole boxes of eggs for four people."

For some reason, the image of Evelyn doing this made us almost laugh, uncomfortably.

"Why?" I asked.

"Well, you know about how Evelyn's mum killed herself? Well schizophrenia runs in the family. Apparently, if it's going to come out, it often starts when you are in your teens."

None of us laughed anymore. We couldn't believe it.

"Her dad had to put Evelyn into an institution!" Elizabeth frowned. "She's not well. They must not watch Evelyn closely because she keeps escaping."

"I thought she was on drugs when she called." I shook my head, still in disbelief. "She sounded wasted."

"Evelyn would never do drugs!" Elizabeth shot back.

"So where is she?" Anna asked. "Can we see her?"

"She's in a psychiatric ward in Darlinghurst. I'm going to visit her this weekend. You guys should come along."

That weekend, we joined Elizabeth and visited Evelyn.

It was Saturday evening and we had planned to attend a dance party at the Hordern later that night. We'd already bought our tickets a week earlier. We were way too dressed up for a visit to a mental hospital. From outside, the building looked like an apartment block. There was no security fence or barbed wire. The building was surrounded with a tiny brick fence that anyone could easily jump over. The only clue that this place was a mental institution was two ambulances parked out front of the brightly lit entrance.

Evelyn's dad was seated in the reception area in an uncomfortable looking plastic chair. I noticed that it was the same type of chair they had inside the Hordern Pavilion for stadium seating around the dance floor. Evelyn's dad was a large Islander man. His chunky legs hung over the chair. He smiled gently at us, glad to see us, but I could see the sadness in his eyes.

"Evelyn. She's not well." He couldn't look any of us directly in the eye when he said this. I think he was ashamed, which he didn't need to be. We all had loved Evelyn as a friend and were not able to reconcile what she was going through. Evelyn's Dad looked like he'd come to the waiting room straight from the construction site where he worked. He held a bright yellow plastic hard hat in his hands.

"Can we see her?" Elizabeth spoke respectfully.

"She's gone." Evelyn's Dad looked embarrassed. "Ran away."

"Escaped?" Elizabeth asked.

Evelyn's Dad nodded.

We looked at each other, not knowing what to do and sat down in the uncomfortable plastic chairs along with Evelyn's Dad and waited. It seemed like ages before another ambulance pulled into the driveway outside the waiting room. The medics opened the backdoor and we saw Evelyn inside. She was dressed in an ill-fitting cotton hospital gown. Her hair was lopsided like she just gotten out of bed. Yet Evelyn had a giant smile on her face when she saw us with her dad in the waiting room.

"Oh, shame!" Evelyn put a hand over her face.

We kind of laughed, glad to see that Evelyn still had her sense of humour. At least she was sane enough to make fun of this situation, to lighten the mood by turning it into a joke as soon as she saw us waiting and the medics helped her exit the ambulance safely.

Anna gave me a worried glance when we saw how wobbly Evelyn was on her feet. The paramedics helped Evelyn walk.

My heart sank as I watched. Evelyn was too young for this to be happening. I caught the look on Elizabeth, Anna, Lee, Simon, and Sarah's faces. They were smiling, happy to see Evelyn. But there was disbelief behind each smile.

We hugged Evelyn and were taken to an ugly grey Visitors Room. Other patients were wandering around the visiting area and it was hard not to look at them. Evelyn was in a place with very mentally ill people. She was one of them, somehow. One man, who looked about twenty years old, was talking to himself, while a woman rocked back and forth, picking things out of the air that weren't there.

Anna had brought Evelyn a gift from her mum, from the local Hare Krishna temple in Darlinghurst. Anna's mum went there regularly to make food to help feed the homeless. When Anna's mum had heard about what had happened to Evelyn, she'd told Anna to take Evelyn a blessed vegetarian meal. "Try this." Anna smiled. "My mum says it will be good for your soul."

Evelyn took one bite and put the food down. "I – can't – taste – any – thing," Evelyn spoke slowly. It was obvious Evelyn was heavily medicated. It must have been something far harder than ecstasy. She couldn't hold a conversation. Her eyes kept closing shut. She looked like she was going to fall asleep and was struggling to stay alert.

Another patient approached us, a tall, pale, skinny middle-aged man with long stringy grey hair. He looked like Steven-the-Eckie-Man and spoke at the same speed Evelyn did now.

"Do – you – mind – if – I – play – ... – the piano?"

"Sure," we answered in unison.

"Thank – you – I – don't – want – ... – to – disturb – you."

Our eyes darted to each other as the man who looked like Steven moved toward an old-fashioned, upright piano in the corner of the room. We watched in silence as he sat on the piano stool ready to play. But all he did was play one single chord, C-major, and that was it. He closed the piano lid, stood up, and walked slowly down the hall.

The woman who had been picking things out of the air raced over to the piano and began to play *Mary had a little lamb*.

I couldn't believe Evelyn was locked up with all these people.

At 9 p.m., we were told we had to leave. Visiting hours were over.

"Please – come – back," Evelyn pleaded. "Don't – forget – me. They – think – I'm – crazy – ... – but – I'm – not! – I – hate – it – in – here..."

I wanted to take her with us. To help Evelyn escape!

We each kissed and hugged Evelyn goodbye and promised to come back to see her again.

As we left the institution, I felt guilty. We were the ones who altered our minds for kicks, while Evelyn, who never went near drugs, never touched ecstasy, had somehow become the one who lost her mind and got locked up.

It was hard to leave Evelyn there. Especially as we were about to go to the Hordern to go mental on acid. That's what we'd been saying and looking forward to all week at school: catching up with Tiffany and taking acid. Then we'd found out about Evelyn's condition. Seeing Evelyn like that should have been a warning about how delicate our minds are, and that experimenting with such powerful and unknown substances was risking our own sanity.

BAD TRIP

AFTER WE SAW Evelyn, we walked through Darlinghurst, past The Wall, and headed up to Paddington towards the Showgrounds. None of us really felt like going to a dance party. Collectively, our mood was low. But since we had paid for our tickets and I'd arranged to hook up with Belinda and Brad to get acid, we went along just the same.

But once we reached the gates, the atmosphere was very different. The crowd waiting to get in was full of yobbos and westies, not the usual cool Paddington dance party crowd. We couldn't find Tiffany outside, so we went in. There were gangs of older kids from the western suburbs dressed in tacky American rapper gear, nylon tracksuits, Run DMC t-shirts, and white Adidas sneakers.

Inside the Hordern, it didn't get any better. There was even a gang of older kids from Dover Heights High who were in year 12, the same boys who'd used to call me a fucking faggot in year 8, like Matt Hardgrave. They were now acting as if they were so cool because they were at a gay dance party.

Matt had the nerve to ask, 'Hey, Nathan, do you know where I can get some E?"

"No, sorry." I shrugged nonchalantly. I wasn't about to help this yobbo, my ex-bully, to have a good time. "No one's taking E anymore — it's all about acid now. See ya!" And I kept walking.

"These parties are no longer underground." Anna rolled her eyes.

"The crowd is totally mainstream!" Sarah agreed.

"Let's get our trips," I said as we headed to the bar to meet Belinda and Brad.

They both gave me a big hug and I handed over $80 and got four gelatin trips in return. We took our trips and continued to dance, unimpressed. Even the DJ was having a hard time getting the thousands of bodies on the dance floor into the usual euphoric state. He played all the classic anthems, but nothing worked. There were hardly any hands in the air. It was like no one's drugs were working and no one could get into it.

"It just isn't happening tonight!" Lee complained an hour after we swallowed the trips.

"Yeah, I don't feel anything at all," Simon agreed.

Two hours later, it became clear that the acid trips weren't working. Not the way my first one had, and the party didn't get any better. Lee, Simon, and Sarah called it a night and went home. For some reason, Anna and I stayed on. We were desperate to have fun and to get our money's worth. But mostly, I think we wanted to forget about Evelyn being in the mental hospital.

All the regulars we bumped into were blaming the recent police drug busts for ruining the party and the fact that there were so many obvious undercover drug cops working the dance party circuit. The good dealers, like Steven-the-Eckie-Man, were nowhere to be seen.

"Maybe we should buy another trip?" Anna suggested.

We found Michael and Sally outside the Hordern. Michael knew a dealer who was selling strong trips and asked if we wanted any. It was like he was becoming a drug dealer from the way he always offered to sell me drugs, which was perfect because I was usually eager to be a customer.

I handed over the last of our money: $40. "I guess this means — we're walking home," I told Anna as Michael took the money we had reserved for a taxi fare.

"Do you think we need drugs to have a good time?" Anna asked half-heartedly.

"Of course!" I said without any humour.

Just the idea of getting high improved our mood.

Michael returned and gave us two gelatin trips. "They're wicked, man!" He grinned with giant black eyeballs. "I've taken two already tonight."

Half an hour after popping the second trip, the world changed. Anna and I began to enjoy the music. People in the crowd were cheering and shouting with enthusiasm again. The fun was back. The second gelatin trip came on at the same time the effects from the first one Anna and I had popped a few hours ago took hold. That's when we realised they weren't duds at all.

The sensation became very intense and a bit scary. I realised that Anna was slowly slipping into a world of her own. Soon she had no idea who she was, or where she was, in a very bad way. She had taken a double-dose of acid for the first time and was hallucinating in a way she never knew was possible. We were both too inexperienced with LSD and didn't know just how much we'd be affected by unknowingly taking a double dose. It was way too much for Anna to handle.

She was totally embarrassing herself, falling over, and wanting to lie down in the middle of the dance floor. Anna wanted to rest under all the people trying to dance around her. She was collapsing onto the discarded empty plastic water bottles that littered the floor along with chewing gum wrappers and grime.

I tried to get her up, but she refused. Even though I was hallucinating and out-of-it, I knew I had to take Anna out of the party for her sake. "Come on, Anna, we're going." I lifted Anna's arms and pulled her body up from the dirty dance floor and dragged her towards the exit.

She was completely disorientated. Unless you knew what she'd taken, it looked like Anna had too much alcohol to drink. We both stupidly got our wrists stamped as we exited the Showgrounds in case we wanted to return. It was a colourful stamp that said, Hordern. It was a seemingly pointless act in hindsight, as Anna would never return to the Hordern.

We exited the gates and bumped into Frieda, the year 9 try-hard goth girl.

"Hi, guys!" Frieda yelled. She was beaming with excitement and acted like we were really good friends.

Anna didn't recognise Frieda at all, even though she was the girl who'd recently asked her in the high school toilet if she could buy ecstasy for her.

Frieda had obviously taken Anna's advice and found where to buy some at the Hordern. Her eyes were rolling and her jaw was clenching as she hugged herself, taking massive deep breaths. "What are you guys on?" Frieda asked.

"Acid," I said. "What are you on?"

"Fantasy." Frieda rubbed her upper body slowly.

Anna pointed at Frieda and giggled. "Are you for real?"

I couldn't let Frieda see Anna acting like this.

"Enjoy it!" I told Frieda and dragged Anna away. "We're leaving. This party isn't any good."

"Are you fucking kidding?" Frieda protested. "It's the best party ever!"

Since it was probably her second or third dance party, maybe it was. For us, we were getting burnt out and the drugs were fucking us up badly.

Seeing Frieda helped Anna regain some perspective on reality. "Yuck! She looked so…horrid! And the way she was moving… Her face looked all twisted! It was like…she was a cheap prostitute trying to come on to you."

I laughed nervously. I had to support Anna to help her walk in a straight line. I knew if I let go she would collapse again.

She slowly stuttered, "God…do – you – think … we – looked – like – that … when – we – took – ecstasy?"

"I hope not!"

We walked up Moore Park Road towards Centennial Park.

Anna shrieked. "All I can see is faces. They're in the leaves! They're in the trees and they have their own expressions with blinking eyes and sharp jagged teeth!"

Suddenly, I could also see faces in the trees, but they didn't look evil. They were incredible and angelic. But I tried not to notice my hallucinations because I was determined to take Anna back to my parents' place so she could come down in a safe place. Hopefully, without my parents twigging to what was going on.

"God, Nathan." Anna breathed heavily. "What if I'm going to be…like this forever! Like Evelyn! You'll have to take care of me forever! My mum can't find out."

"Anna, you're going to be fine!" I said as much for my benefit as for Anna's. I had to concentrate to think about which direction we needed to walk to get home. Even though it was my neighbourhood, I barely recognised where I was. The acid trip was making me delirious, but I held on to normality as hard as I could for Anna. "Don't worry, Anna, it will wear off by the time we walk back to my house. Try and enjoy it while it lasts."

But as we walked past Centennial Park towards my parents' home, Anna continued to get worse and could not walk a single step without assistance.

I had no clue what we were going to do once we got back to my place. I fumbled to get my key in the door. All I could see in the dark was glittery sparks flying out of the keyhole. "I'm fucked," I whispered. I could barely focus on opening the front door as Anna collapsed on the doormat.

I finally managed to unlock the door and it creaked open. I picked up Anna off the doormat. She was limp like a rag doll. "Don't make a sound!" I whispered.

I led Anna inside and closed the door. I headed straight for my bedroom. In the darkness, I could hear Dad snoring from my parents' bedroom as we crept up the stairs. Luckily, both my parents were sound asleep, and Anna kept quiet.

I rested Anna on my bed and closed the door. "Anna?" I whispered. "Are you ok?"

She didn't respond. She looked unconscious.

"Anna?"

She nodded slowly but looked miles away.

I paced back and forth in my bedroom and kept looking at Anna, not knowing what to do.

"Can I…stay here…until it…wears off?" Anna whispered.

To my relief, she sounded more like herself again. "For sure! Stay here. I'm going to get you some food maybe that will help you feel normal." I closed my bedroom door and came face-to-face with my mother, and I inhaled deeply with surprise.

"You're home?" Mum sounded surprised and looked half asleep as she blinked against the light, giving me a suspicious look.

In that instant, it hit me how unusual it must be for a mother to say this at 4:30 a.m. on a Sunday morning.

Even though the acid had altered every single brain cell I had, I knew that Mum sensed that something was wrong. *Act normal*, I told myself. "Party was no good." I shrugged and walked towards the kitchen to lead Mum away from my bedroom door. I couldn't risk her discovering Anna in the state she was in. We'd be busted badly. "I'm going to get some food and go to bed." I pretended to yawn as Mum followed me downstairs into the kitchen.

I tried to act like I wasn't tripping. I tried not to be alarmed by the melting walls, the swaying fridge, and the dancing toaster.

Luckily, Mum was half asleep and she didn't notice how out-of-it I was.

I stared at an empty bowl for nearly a minute before remembering I needed to add corn flakes to make breakfast.

"I think you've been over doing all this dance party business, Nathan." Mum yawned. "I don't know how you do it! When I was your age, 'dances,' as we used to call them, ended at midnight. They didn't go on all night like they do these days."

"Times change." I shrugged, grabbed a spoon, and opened the fridge door. Everything inside the refrigerator came alive. The vegetables were throbbing and the left-over roast chicken was calling my name. *Where's the milk?* I began to panic.

"Close it before the food spoils!" Mum sounded annoyed.

I looked at Mum. She looked tired and unhappy. She made me feel bad. She didn't know me at all. But I couldn't think about it for too long. I had to get rid of Mum to take care of Anna. "Sorry I woke you, Mum. You should go back to bed. You look like you need some sleep."

"I wouldn't look like this if you didn't wake me up in the middle of the night," Mum said before she headed back to bedroom. "You get yourself to bed, young man."

As she left, I let out an enormous sigh of relief. My heart was racing. I took the bowl of corn flakes and a glass of orange juice back to my bedroom. Anna was in the same position on my bed, dressed in psychedelic dance party cloths and looking miserable. I placed the bowl on the bedside table and gently shook Anna's shoulder. She moved slowly. I tried to get her to eat the corn flakes with little success.

After putting one spoonful in her mouth, Anna chewed for a second, looked confused and gave up. An image of how Evelyn had done the same thing earlier in the evening when Anna had offered her Hare Krishna food at the mental institution flashed through my mind. "It tastes like…nothing." Anna looked at me with alarm. "Oh my God, what if I can't taste anything ever again?"

A few hours later, light crept into my room beneath the curtains as the sun started to rise. I knew that I'd either have to talk to my parents about what was really going on or somehow sneak Anna out of the house before they got up. If I let Anna stay at my place, her mum would know something was up. Her mum would probably think that Anna and I were sleeping together! In a way, Anna was lucky I was a closet gay. Any other boy from school would have taken advantage of Anna if she were in this state, on their bed.

"Anna, pull it together," my voice was edgy. "The best thing you can do now is to go home, go to bed and sleep it off."

"No. Please don't make me go home," Anna pleaded. "I can't! My mum will know!"

"But if you stay here, your Mum will think something else is going on! She's going to think we're doing it!"

Anna considered this and looked even more concerned. "Okay," she agreed reluctantly. "I guess I do sort of feel better now."

I grabbed the last $20 from my money box and called a taxi from the portable phone in my bedroom and snuck Anna out. We crept out of my bedroom, down the stairs and out the front door. I rode in the taxi with Anna back to her apartment block in Paddington. Anna seemed fine as the taxi zipped through the empty Sunday morning streets. She was a little weary but, most importantly, no longer freaking out.

"Thanks for taking care of me." Anna gave me a peck on the cheek when she got out of the taxi. "If you hadn't been around, I don't know what would have happened to me."

"You'll be okay. If you go straight to bed and don't come out until you feel normal again. Otherwise, your mum's going to work it out."

Anna nodded that she understood.

I was so relieved she'd come back to reality.

"See you tomorrow at the bus stop." Anna smiled and slammed the taxi door shut.

I asked the driver to wait for Anna to enter the apartment block. Once she was inside, I let out a deep breath feeling like we'd gotten away with it. I also felt so over it. So sick of what was going on. Were we still having fun? Didn't feel like it.

Never again, I vowed. *Last night was it. Last time I take drugs!*

MOTHER'S DAY

I CAME HOME FOR the second time at 6:30 a.m. on Sunday morning and snuck back into the house. I went to bed and lay there for a while before I drifted into a nervous twitchy sleep that didn't last for long.

"Nathan! Nathan! Wake up!" Mum was holding the portable phone looking anxious. "It's Anna's mother!" She handed me the phone. "She wants a word with you!"

I suddenly became very awake. "Hello?"

"This is Eva," Anna's Mum spoke with a heavy European accent. "Anna, she's gone *crazy*!" Eva emphasised the word crazy, so it really did sound crazy.

In the background, I could hear sounds of someone wailing, like a little girl, only it wasn't a little girl, it was Anna.

Anna called out, "Don't let them get me!"

"What happened?" Eva was stern. It sounded like Eva already knew.

I didn't know what to say with my Mum and Dad standing by my bedside, listening to my every word. I couldn't pretend any longer. I had to come clean to help Anna.

"What's going on, Nathan?" Dad looked angry.

There was nothing I could do to get Anna and me out of this without getting into trouble. So, I pulled out the oldest excuse every recreational drug user does when they get sprung. "I think someone put something in Anna's drink," I mumbled.

"What?" Eva voice was as sharp as she was to the point.

"I think Anna's drink got spiked," I said more convincingly.

"What with?" Eva didn't sound surprised.

"Acid."

As I said it, I saw my parents' faces turn a shade of white. Mum's jaw dropped and Dad shook his head with disappointment.

"*Acid?*" Eva sounded confused.

"LSD" I called it what I knew Anna's mum and my parents would have known the drug as when they were younger, having lived through the sexual revolution in the late 1960s when half the planet turned on, tuned in, and dropped out.

"Oh." There was a long pause from Eva on the end of the phone line. "I see. Thank you for telling me." Eva didn't say goodbye. She just hung up and I was left with my parents looking at me like I was a mass murderer.

I pressed the disconnect button.

"What's going on?" Mum looked mortified.

"You bloody better not to be taking drugs!" Dad fumed.

"I—," I didn't know what else to say. So many times, I had wanted to tell my parents what was really going on, thinking it would be so much better if they could understand how excellent dance parties and ecstasy were or that I was gay, hoping they could understand. But by the time my Mum and Dad finally asked if I was taking drugs, it was no longer a good thing, and I wasn't having a good time.

I looked at Mum and Dad. I was still tripping, and the air swirled around their faces. It was like I could read their auras. Red. Angry. "No! I'm not on drugs!" I lied. "It's like I said, someone spiked Anna's drink!" There was so much I wished I could tell them but knew there was no way they could handle what I had to say. They weren't ready to hear about how I was gay, or that my idea of a good time was dancing till dawn on ecstasy or LSD with several thousand people.

"Why the bloody hell didn't you tell us what happened to Anna?"

Dad didn't let me off this time. "For God's sake, anything could have happened to her. She could have died!"

The gravity of what had happened hit me. It was the last thing I needed as the effects of coming down from two trips kicked in. I pulled the covers over my face and hid under the blankets in the darkness.

"Some Mother's Day this has turned out to be," Mum said and left my bedroom.

"Hope you're satisfied with yourself!" Dad said leaving me alone to wonder when and how did it all get so out of control.

In the afternoon, I woke up in a cold sweat. It was officially the worst Mother's Day of all time, and I was the worst son in the world. I couldn't believe I had forgotten it was Mother's Day. Somehow, I gotten distracted with the dance party scene, Evelyn going mad, and now Anna losing the plot. I started to think that I was going to be next.

I grabbed the portable phone and dialed Anna's number. I had to check she was okay! I was nervous about the possibility of having to speak to Anna's mum again.

"Hello?" Eva answered the phone.

"Hi," I pretended like nothing had happened, like everything was back to normal. "Can I speak to Anna?" As I spoke, I realised I was still tripping. There were patterns bubbling across my bedroom walls. *How long does this stuff work for?* I wondered as I waited for Eva to put Anna on the phone.

Anna came on and said, "Hello?"

I was overjoyed to hear Anna sounding okay. "Thank God you're all right."

"All right," Anna suddenly sounded strange. "What do you mean?"

"Anna?"

"Everything's just like floating away."

I heard the telephone receiver on Anna's end slam against the floor. "Anna can you hear me?" There was no response.

All I could hear was Anna somewhere in the background. "Mum, it's happening again!"

"It comes in waves," Eva sounded annoyed in the distance. "You're going through another phase. It will pass. Calm down!"

"Where am I?" Anna asked. Anna sounded more mental than Evelyn had in the mental institution.

"You're having another hallucination," Eva said reassuringly.

I listened to my best friend hallucinate for a few more minutes before I felt like I was invading her privacy. Also, I realised that Anna had totally forgotten I was waiting on the line for her to come back. I was scared Anna wasn't coming back mentally either, as I hung up, feeling freaked out.

I spent the remainder of Sunday afternoon avoiding my parents and phoned Lee to tell him about Anna.

"Shit, man!" Lee's voice was filled with concern. "Is she going to be okay?"

"I don't know." I hated to admit it. "It doesn't sound good."

By Sunday evening, I still hadn't heard from Anna. She was all I could think about. I had to find out if she was better. So, I phoned one more time. Again, Eva answered the phone. This time, I asked Eva if Anna was better.

"No. She is still…sick."

ADVANCE AUSTRALIA FAIR

FELT SICK ON Monday morning when Anna didn't show up at the bus station. I sat with Lee, Simon, and Sarah in stone-cold silence as the school bus lurched back and forth towards Dover Heights High. We gave each other looks of concern as the bus made its way to school, stopping every five minutes and filling up with more kids. Everyone else was shouting and talking about what they got up to on the weekend.

I was sure none of their friends had overdosed on LSD.

When we arrived for rollcall, to our surprise, inside the school auditorium, we found Anna standing in line, dressed in a freshly ironed school uniform.

Anna smiled when she saw us.

We raced to Anna and gave her a big hug.

"Are you ok?" I asked.

"I'm fine," Anna answered.

"Why weren't you at the bus stop?" Sarah asked.

"My mum dropped me off. She wanted to make sure I got to school ok and didn't," Anna lowered her voice so no one else could hear, "didn't try to take more acid trips on my way to school." She laughed nervously and we all burst into laughter, releasing the tension left hanging over us following the weekend. "I'll tell you guys what happened after rollcall," Anna said, as more students filled the auditorium. She still looked edgy and didn't want anyone else to know what had happened or suspect anything.

Before we could say another word, the Deputy Principal, Mrs Harris, interrupted us. "Attention! Attention students! Please stand for the National Anthem."

We stood facing the stage as a scratchy recording of Advance Australia Fair, the operatic, symphonic mix, began to play.

For once, we didn't have to endure the whole recording. There was a loud thump sound, like someone had fainted. The sound was someone's head hitting the auditorium floorboards. Every head turned to take a better look.

Lee, Simon, Sarah, and I immediately looked in Anna's direction.

But she was standing tall and looking back at us with surprise. This was not another hallucination! Someone else had passed out.

Mrs Harris took the microphone and called for everyone to settle down.

Mr Caldwell, the school's wood-shop teacher, and Mr Knight, our math's teacher, moved quickly to the centre of the auditorium.

"Give her some space!" Mr Caldwell yelled at the students as he took the arms and Mr Knight grabbed the legs and lifted a seemingly lifeless body.

Standing on my toes to get a better look, I saw the body in Mr Caldwell's arms. It was Frieda, the year 9 goth girl, the one who had been on fantasy when Anna and I had fled the Hordern on Saturday night. Frieda was white as a ghost. She was out cold and had no idea the entire school could see her undies as she was carried out of the school hall.

"There must be some really bad drugs going around town." Lee was the first to comment on what had just happened, after school assembly.

"Poor girl," Anna felt sorry for Frieda. It was too close to what she'd just been through. Anna told us how she had come out of the trip at around 9:30 p.m. on Sunday night. "Turns out, my mum knows all about LSD. She tried it in the 1970s. But when she did it, she was in her twenties, not a teenager. Mum told me about how she and

Dad had dropped acid before they were married. They did it totally different to the way we did. They went to a cabin in Switzerland with friends, food supplies, and a guide."

"A guide?" Simon asked.

"Yeah, the guide was there to assist them to appreciate the journey and expand their consciousness. When they took acid, it was for spiritual enlightenment, not for partying."

"I can't believe your mum told you all this," I said.

"We had a deep talk once I came out of it. After you dropped me off, I was convinced I was going to die and made my mum call an ambulance. When they saw the Hordern stamp on my wrist they were like, *'typical'*. They told my mum they had seen a lot of this lately. They didn't even give me anything to calm down, they told my mum I had to ride it out. And when they were checking my vital signs, I was convinced they were aliens. I was hallucinating so badly that I thought I'd been taken on board a UFO and they were performing tests on me!"

"Shit!" Sarah said as the second bell for first period rang.

We ignored it and continued to listen to Anna recounting her ordeal.

"For most of the afternoon, I thought I was God and that the view out my window was a universe I had created." Suddenly Anna turned very serious, "I'm never allowed out again. Mum and I had a big talk last night. I told her everything that's been going on."

Both Sarah and Lee's jaw dropped.

"Don't worry," Anna assured them. "I made Mum promise she wouldn't tell any of your parents."

"What did she say?" I asked, curious.

"She couldn't believe how fast I had grown up in the last year. Mum said she hadn't seen it coming and had no idea what was happening. She was so wonderful the way she stayed with me through the trip. She never got angry, she stayed calm, and I think it saved me from going off the edge."

"I'm so glad you're all right!" Sarah gave Anna another hug.

"You know, I think my bad trip happened for a reason," Anna said.

"What do you mean?" I looked at her, confused.

"It was like we were moving too fast. Something serious had to happen to make me stop and think about what I was doing."

WORK EXPERIENCE?

I N THE FINAL week of the term two of year 11, we were meant to be doing work experience. Everyone in year 11 got assigned work placement positions by our career's councilor, Mr McCoy. I got placed at the local Paddington community radio station because I had expressed an interest in becoming a journalist. But instead of turning up, I faked a sickie that lasted a whole week, and used the work experience week as an excuse to catch up with Tiffany and go clubbing like it was my full-time occupation. Since she'd returned to Australia, I hadn't really seen her much and in that time a lot had happened.

"I've dropped out of school!" Tiffany announced with pride. "My life is so good now. I'm working as a waitress at one of the coolest cafés on Oxford Street."

"No way!" I was so jealous. "What did your mum say?"

"She was spewing at first, but she got over it." Tiffany sounded like someone who'd won a personal victory. "Nathan, you have to come out with me. I've become a regular at The Vault. It's the new downstairs bar of The Exchange."

That night, I met up with Tiffany at the Oxford Street café where she now worked. She gave me a free coffee while I waited for her to finish her shift. Then we headed down to where it had all started, The Exchange.

"The old Exchange is tragic now," Tiffany warned me. "That's why everyone goes to the new downstairs bar, The Vault. I've got member-ship, so we'll get in without any hassles."

Everyone inside The Vault seemed to know Tiffany, from the door bitch to the bar staff, and Eddie, who was Tiffany's drug dealer. Tif-fany promptly scored two trips, which we popped together in the girls' toilet. For some reason, Tiffany's dealer looked familiar to me. I was sure I'd seen him before at the Hodern Pavilion.

Tiffany said, "I only go to places like The Vault now because I don't have to pay a cover charge and they play good music all night long." As the trips came on, Tiffany convinced me that the reason she only went to clubs was because, "People who go to dance parties at the Hordern are so uncool. Dance parties have gotten so commercial. All the cool party people are back in the clubs again!"

I loved being back on the dance floor with Tiffany. I gave her a hug. "It's the same as being at a big dance party but on a smaller scale."

I didn't realise the truth behind Tiffany's return to clubbing. It was because she couldn't afford to pay $40 a ticket for the Hordern dance parties anymore. The $40 ticket would have left no money for drugs. And drugs had become essential to having a good time.

"We're so alike," Tiffany smiled. "That's why I love you so much, Nathan."

"I know. We'll be best friends for life!" I smiled with complete sincerity as we both hallucinated on LSD.

As the work experience week turned into school holidays, I got wasted every second night with Tiffany. By the time I'd begun to recover from the previous night's outing, Tiffany wanted me to go out with her to do it all over again.

My parents gave up on lecturing me about how I was throwing my life away. They were tired of my behavior, and warned me that I was going to end up a 'no hoper.' They couldn't understand why I insisted on going out all the time. I assured them I knew what I was doing; it wasn't as bad as they thought it was.

I said, "Come on. It's school holidays!"

"But you're too young to be going out all the time!" Dad yelled at me, frustrated because he just couldn't get through.

The more I went out, the more I started to see my parents as a means to an end. By the end of the first week of school holidays, I had used up all my savings on drugs. But I didn't care. I was having way too much fun.

The only problem was that I had no money left to go out. Unlike Tiffany, I didn't work full-time. But I didn't let this stop me from going out. I had no choice but to steal $50 from my mum's purse. I felt shitty for doing it. It was incredibly low. But I knew there was no way Mum would have given it to me if I had asked for it.

It only took several months for me to reach a stage where I felt I had no choice but to go out all the time. Going out was all I could think about. It was all I wanted to do. I couldn't miss out on it.

The night I stole the $50 note was a bad one. It was like instant karma hit me for the fight I'd had with Mum when I left the house. The worst thing imaginable happened. The dealer Tiffany gave our money to ripped us off. He was meant to give us speed. But when Tiffany opened the satchel of powder in a toilet cubicle of The Vault, she soon realised that what she'd paid $100 for was nothing more than icing sugar.

"Fuck!" Tiffany screamed at the top of her lungs when she realised we'd been duped.

"There's no refund when it comes to drugs." I tried to lighten the mood.

Tiffany and I looked at each other with horror. We had no money and no drugs. How were we supposed to have a good time?

"No way!" Tiffany banged the toilet cubicle wall with frustration.

Tiffany and I decided to leave The Vault. There was no point in being there unless we were out-of-it. We had to find a way to get something. We walked through Kings Cross, past the strip joints, the junkies, the prostitutes, and the crowds of people out just like us, looking for a good time.

"I can't believe it!" This was all Tiffany could say over and over as we walked together in a bad mood.

"I'm not freaked out about losing the $50," I told Tiffany. "I'm more freaked out because we have no drugs for tonight!" As we walked, I looked at Tiffany and vividly remembered the great times we'd spent together before we knew what illicit drugs were. It had only been a year ago that we were fifteen years old and all it had taken was a bottle of Jim Beam and some Coke to make us happy. Now, alcohol was a thing of the past; no one got drunk anymore. It was so pre-pubescent. Just a year on and we both needed much stronger stuff to turn things from bad to good, from boring to fun, from sober to cool again.

Tiffany felt so guilty because it was her dealer who'd fucked up that she got another $100 out of her savings account. It was all she had left.

Tiffany took me to a place called the Kardomah Cafe. It was a dodgy underground club on Bayswater Road in Kings Cross. The entire club was as big as one of the classrooms at Dover. Only it was painted completely black, with flashing lights and was free and easy to get into. At midnight, the Kardomah was virtually empty inside. Only a few deadbeats were on the dance floor and the music was shit.

I could imagine all the cool people having a good time at the Hordern Pavilion. How had I come to this, spending my night in such a shady part of town? "This is crap!" I said in disbelief. "Seriously, can this night get any worse?"

"Relax. This place will come alive when *Site* closes at 2 a.m. That's when Eddie, my regular dealer, will be here," Tiffany explained. "I can't believe that other guy ripped us off."

It was so sad being the only two cool people inside the Kardomah Cafe.

By 2.30 a.m., Tiffany spotted Eddie, the dealer she'd been waiting for. He looked tough, had a crew cut, and wore a black nylon padded bomber jacket that had white cotton letters sown on the back, reading, In Full Effect. I'd seen guys wearing these jackets before at the

Hordern. In fact, he was the guy Steven-the-Eckie-Man scored pills from for us once when Steven had run out of pills.

Tiffany told Eddie about how we'd been ripped off earlier.

"Man! That sucks." Eddie frowned. "Make sure you look out for me next time."

Tiffany bought two Utopia capsules from Eddie, and we wasted no time popping them into our mouths and swallowing them with water directly from the bathroom tap.

Half an hour later, I felt like I could do cartwheels across the tiny dance floor. The music was far better suddenly. It was like the DJ had discovered a secret stash of the best tracks. Tiffany and I were even able to smile once more.

"Do you realise that tonight cost us $200 on drugs alone?" Tiffany laughed like this was the funniest thing ever.

I was so high on Utopia that this now seemed funny. For the next half hour, I couldn't stop giggling at the thought of how much money we'd wasted. Even for Eastern suburbs teenage kids, $200 was a small fortune.

Eddie danced with us for a while. He moved really fast, like he had sampled his own merchandise. It turned out Eddie was part of a bigger group of dealers. The Kardomah Cafe was where they all came to hang out once they'd sold their stuff. Suddenly, there were another four guys wearing the same black nylon padded bomber jackets with In Full Effect written on the back. It was their very own unique, branded drug dealership slogan and they wore it with pride.

This group of dealers looked nothing like Steven-the-Eckie-Man. They weren't middle-aged, burnt-out drug-freaks. They were all in their late-teens and early-twenties. They wore Doc Martin shoes and Levi jeans with their branded bomber jackets. These guys were good looking. But they weren't gay. Or at least, they weren't as far as I could tell.

I was reminded how straight they were when Eddie got onto Tiffany. Suddenly, they tongue kissed and rubbed up against each other as I kept dancing, acting like I didn't care.

The In Full Effect crew took drugs, dealt drugs, and danced all night on drugs. They were the new breed of straight boys on the edge. They seemed so much more experienced than Tiffany and me. I felt cool just hanging out with them. Eddie was twenty-one-years old. To me he seemed so grown up. I couldn't believe that by the end of the night we were hanging out with the In Full Effect crew.

When the Kardomah Cafe closed at 6 a.m., Eddie invited Tiffany and me back to his place to crash. "If you want to come down at our pad, it's cool." He shrugged nonchalantly.

"Okay." Tiffany and I didn't even have to think about our answer.

"We'll probably keep going all day." Eddie grinned.

HIGH ALL THE TIME

THE IN FULL Effect crew rented a five-bedroom terrace house in Darlinghurst, a few blocks walk away from the Kardomah Cafe. The next morning, Tiffany and I sat rolling around in fits of laughter in their tiny living room, recovering from dancing all night. The TV was on in the background with the sound turned down. House music pumped from the stereo as Eddie passed around a bong and a bottle of amyl nitrate.

On the TV, an Australian Government Drug Offensive commercial came on. The advertisement was about the dangers of heroin. Even though heroin wasn't relevant to us party people, for some reason, we all took notice of the commercial and burst into laughter.

"I hate that commercial; it's so dumb!" Tiffany moaned as the TV showed a young man walking into a toilet cubicle. Inside, the man finds two young men holding a needle and a tourniquet about to shoot up. The two guys offer the young man a hit. And as they do, subtitles replace what the guys say with warning messages about how dangerous and deadly sharing needles is. The young man declines their offer for a hit.

For laughs, Eddie and Baz re-enacted the commercial. Eddie pretended to be the guy walking into a toilet cubicle and Baz was one of the guys about to shoot up.

"Would you like some?" Baz offered Eddie an invisible needle.

"Would you risk infection of HIV or Hep B?" Eddie used his fingers to slice through the air pretending to read an imaginary subtitle.

Everyone in the living room cracked up laughing.

"It won't hurt you," Baz repeated the lines from the anti-drug ad word for word.

"Yeah, sure, Baz. It may even kill you," Eddie put on a serious news reporter voice.

The serious anti-drug message became a big joke when we were coming down from a night of hard drug taking. It was the funniest thing I'd ever seen as we passed around a little brown bottle.

"As if people just give away free drugs in the toilet!" Eddie laughed.

"Such a waste of taxpayers' money. The government has no idea!" Baz scoffed as the living room began to spin from the fumes of the amyl nitrate.

Eddie kept paying out on the anti-drug commercial, making us laugh. "It may even kill you. Ha, Ha!"

Tears rolled down Tiffany's face from laughing too hard. For these guys, everything was a joke, including death and disease. This was the level the In Full Effect crew partied on. They had no boundaries. All that mattered was getting out-of-it and staying out-of-it. The point wasn't to crash, or come down, but to keep going, to prolong the high to the point where they didn't come down at all. They kept going until the next night and then did it all over again. They were high all the time.

I got home at 4 p.m. the next afternoon. School holidays were a traumatic time for my parents. I knew that my Mum had probably been fighting fears, thinking about the possibility that I might be dead. She'd probably had to resist the urge to phone the police this time. Part of me did feel guilty when I saw Mum looking so stressed-out when I finally came home, but then, what could I do about it? It was my life. I was living my life how I wanted. At sixteen, I thought I was pretty much a grown-up and didn't think my parents had any right to tell me what I could or couldn't do.

I told Mum that this was what all my friends were doing. But the truth was that no one else from The Group, or any other group from my school, were doing what I was doing. They were studying for the HSC. Even my best friends didn't really know what I was doing with Tiffany.

Mum told me I wasn't allowed out ever again. "You're overdoing it!" she yelled angrily.

"You can't control me!" I yelled back. "I swear I will drop out of high school, just like Tiffany, if you try to stop me!" I knew the last thing my parents wanted was for me to drop out of school. So they had no choice but to accept that, on holidays, it was my time to party hard.

But partying hard left me feeling worse for wear. When I came down off acid and ecstasy at my parents' home, I could no longer stand how horrible I felt. Coming down and being alone in my bedroom, suddenly it all seemed so meaningless. I couldn't sleep, yet I was exhausted. I was intelligent enough to know that what I was doing was so pointless. Yet, I kept doing it. The thought I was flirting with addiction never crossed my drug-fueled, teenage mind.

That's why I preferred to come down with Tiffany at the In Full Effect crew's place. It didn't feel so bad when I came down with people who were doing the same thing. It was fun when I was with people who were in the same ecstatic state. At the crew's place, we paid out on each other and laughed at how tragic we looked until we passed out. It was better than being alone in my single bed, thinking about how there was no point to life, feeling that there was no way I could return to being just a high school student after the school holidays.

When I came home all I could think about was how confused I felt. I didn't know why I kept finding myself in the same, unhappy situation. After having had the very best time of my life the night before, I totally regretted it the next day. But as soon as day turned to night, when I got a phone call from Tiffany, I was set to do it all over again, desperate to get out of my parents' house, desperate to have a good time, even though I'd barely had two hours sleep, nor really eaten much. I was ready to dance all night, non-stop just one more time.

I thought the In Full Effect crew were the biggest group of drug dealers operating in the inner-city club scene. They had totally infiltrated the Sydney dance party circuit and I felt profoundly cool to hang out with them. And it wasn't like they forced me, or Tiffany, to take drugs or do anything sinister.

Eddie just wanted us to hang out with them. He even gave us advice on what drugs to buy and which ones to avoid, because they were of lesser quality. The In Full Effect crew only sold the lesser quality drugs to the one-offs, the people they didn't recognise, the first timers who didn't know any better. A lot of their customers fell into that category.

On Friday night, before the school holidays ended, Tiffany and I met up at The Vault where we popped a trip and danced till 2 a.m. Then we met the crew at the Kardomah Cafe. As soon as we arrived, we dropped a Utopia pill. We were more out-of-it than we'd ever been in our entire life. The only safe place for us to be was on the dance floor, moving to the relentlessly repetitive hypnotic house beat.

We spent the next hour on the dance floor, fully going off to the music, dancing with all the people I'd met at dance parties, moving to one hundred and thirty beats per minute. Collectively we were together, but individually were each in our own little drug-fueled world.

In my drug-fueled world, I knew I was the best dancer in the club. I was showing the world how cool I was on the dance floor. It was so hot that people were stripping off their tops to cool down, baring flesh. I found myself dancing with my bare chest and Tiffany danced only wearing her bra and mini skirt.

We sweated like crazy but loved every second and felt better than ever before. Too out-of-it to think about taking a break, I became oblivious to the heat until my legs trembled, and a sharp pain shot through my abdomen and stomach. My body had overheated. I nearly collapsed. Then I blacked out for a split second. I stopped dancing and stood frozen after having danced non-stop for two hours. I'd sweated a gallon of fluid, along with the other hundred or so drug-fucked people in the tiny dive club. It looked like everyone had taken a shower, fully dressed. The air conditioning must have broken down, yet all the patrons kept dancing like their life depended on it as the music played on relentlessly.

Without saying a word to Tiffany, or anyone else in the crew, I pushed my way off the crowded dance floor, doubled over in pain, and headed for the toilets.

I tripped and fell over. Some strangers helped me up.

I rushed for the toilets and felt like I was going to die.

As I pushed the 'men's' room door open, Tiffany was suddenly behind me, bouncing along happily.

"You going to do some more drugs?" She took my hand, smiling like a five-year-old about to open presents on Christmas morning. Tiffany was too wasted to notice that I had turned white and was fighting the urge to pass out.

I could barely focus on where I was. The bathroom tiles glowed like they were radioactive. I was burning up. I saw a sink and splashed water over my face. I put my mouth under the tap and gulped a liter of water. I didn't care who saw me drink directly from the grimy men's room tap. In the corroded mirror above the basin, I saw a thin young man with dark circles under his bulging eyes. As the eyes stared back, I realised they were mine. My eyes were giant dark hollow holes, dilated pupils swimming in illegal chemicals.

If it was true what religious people said about the eyes being the windows to the soul, mine were nothing more than a dark empty space.

"I'm so skinny," I murmured looking at my gaunt anorexic frame. Only I wasn't anorexic. I have never dieted in my life. I just hadn't eaten much during the school holidays. I had no appetite from constantly coming down from my now regular diet of designer drugs.

Tiffany rested her skinny pale arm around my shoulder. Her eyes were bulging like mine as she chewed gum manically. She was dressed in a black lace bra and mini skirt with fishnet stockings. Her waterproof make-up was smudged; it had melted down her face from the heat on the dance floor. "We look so good!" Tiffany was completely hallucinating, thinking we looked fantastic.

Our reflection in the mirror reminded me of how the prostitutes that worked The Wall near Oxford Street looked. I started to panic. We looked just like those teenagers, the ones who waited on the street for cars to come by and pick them up. In that instant, without any warning, a fluorescent green projectile vomit gushed from my lips like a fire hose. The chemical cocktail contents of my stomach landed on the men's room floor.

"Oh my god!" Tiffany gasped. "Are you okay?"

It had happened so suddenly. I was so wasted that vomiting didn't even feel bad. I did it again. It came out with incredible force and was bright green. It was quick, unexpected, and painless.

There was a small line of clubbers waiting to use the cubicles. Their jaws gaped in disgust.

"Gross!" One guy screwed his face and left the men's room.

"Do you need a doctor?" another one asked.

"I – I don't think so," I stammered. Even I was amazed that I could vomit like that. I guess I spewed up whatever it was that hadn't agreed with me.

Tiffany was so high, she laughed. "Seriously, are you okay?"

"Yeah," I lied. I was far from okay.

What really surprised me was that out of the line of people who'd witnessed me projectile vomit, not even one had reconsidered their decision to go into a toilet cubicle to do more drugs. It was so obvious that the only reason they were lining up, chewing gum, and bopping nervously on the spot, was because they were going to do some more lines or pop another pill behind the closed door.

Tiffany led me back to the dance floor.

My heart was racing. My blood was speeding toxins through my veins and my mind was all over the place. Suddenly, everyone looked like demented Japanese Manga cartoon characters, especially Eddie and Tiffany as they wrapped their arms around each other, nuzzling and kissing like rainbow fish.

I wanted to scream. But instead, I acted calm, pretended to be cool as I listened to the crew talk about a pile of rubbish. Their conversation turned to how close ecstasy makes you feel.

Eddie was saying that when he was younger, around fourteen-years-old, and had started popping pills like E, he used to think he might be gay because he just wanted to hug his mates. But then he'd realised it was just the drug and he wasn't really a faggot.

I grew paranoid. Was Eddie saying that because he knew I was secretly gay? I felt so uncomfortable. I wanted to leave, but I couldn't go anywhere in the state I was in. My eyes wandered to the dance floor. It was packed with all the no-name faces I'd grown to love and recognise from the dance party and club scene. They were all such great friends of mine. Best friends, when on drugs. Yet I knew hardly anything about any of them other than they liked to dance and take drugs. That's what we all had in common. Other than that, I had no idea who these people were! Just as they had no idea who I really was: a closet-gay high school student pretending to be a straight guy two years older than my real age.

Tiffany broke my blurry thoughts. She gave me a hug and placed something in my hand underneath the table. It was half a pill. "It's ecstasy."

I knew it was stupid to take another pill having just vomited, but I was so far out of my head that I had no better judgement than to take it. It seemed like the right thing to do. As I swallowed the bitter tasting pill, Eddie and Tiffany stood on the bar table and started dancing.

"There's not enough room on the dance floor," Tiffany screamed with excitement.

Within minutes, Eddie and Tiffany were told by the security guard to get down.

"That's your last warning mate!" the steroid bloated security guard bellowed.

"Oooooh!" the crew crooned mischievously from around the table, mocking the burly security guard.

I felt like I was back in high school. It reminded me of mucking up in class and getting told off by the teacher.

HARD STUFF

AT 6 A.M., the music stopped, and the lights came on, but the patrons in the Kardomah Cafe were way too out-of-it to go home. Another night had come and gone and some of the people still left on the dance floor didn't notice the club was closing and continued to dance, still in their own special happy little world.

"Club's closed!" yelled the security guards as they booted the remaining patrons out onto the street.

We wandered up through the heart of Kings Cross and headed back to Eddie's place to spend the rest of the day tripping and waiting for each hour of the day to disappear into nightfall. On the way, Eddie asked us if we were going to Base nightclub tonight.

"That's another twelve hours away!" I shrugged, "I'm way too out-of-it to think that far ahead." With every step I took, I could feel I was starting to come down. The ecstasy had worn off, the acid was fading into mild visual hallucinations, and the buzz had disappeared. I was slipping back into reality.

Inside the dirty rented terrace, Eddie passed around a bong. We got totally stoned; it brought back the sensation of last night's drugs and the crew talked about The Cure's new record, *Disintegration*.

Baz put it on the stereo. "Listen to this intro. It's mind blowing."

I listened to the words The Cure's lead singer, Robert Smith, sung, and I felt that he was singing about me, drifting towards the edge of society.

Tiffany smiled at me for a second as she cuddled up to Eddie.

I felt like leaving. I wanted to get out of this place. I felt totally alone, even though the living room was filled with other guys coming down from last night. My fingers fidgeted uncomfortably with the shoelace on my Doc Martin boots. I no longer wanted to be here. But I was too out-of-it to leave by myself. So, I got up and went to the bathroom, let out a gallon of bright yellow fluid, washed my hands in the basin that hadn't been cleaned in months and splashed water over my face.

"Wow," I said to my reflection, "you're completely drug fucked." No wonder it was so easy for me to get into clubs. At sixteen years old, I'd partied so hard that I looked at least twenty years of age.

Opposite the bathroom was a door that led to a small backyard. I went outside to get some air. It was cold outside and there was a gate that opened onto a laneway. I opened the gate and stood next to a stinking garbage bin and a row of parked cars. I didn't know where I was, but knew it was better than what was going on inside the crew's place.

I walked down the alleyway, wasted and alone. I knew it wasn't like the crew would miss me. They were all wasted, and I'd had enough. It was time to leave.

And this was the only way I could do it: without saying a word to any of them, especially Tiffany. This was the only way they would have let me go. I left Tiffany there. She wanted to be there. Next time I saw her, I could pretend I had said goodbye but none of them, including Tiffany, would remember because they were all so out-of-it.

The laneway led to Darlinghurst Road. Walking alone, I felt like an alien that didn't fit into human society. I wished the people on the street couldn't see me. The 'normal people' getting on with their day moved to the opposite side of the pavement to avoid me when I passed, acting like I was some sort of diseased, contagious, homeless street kid. I could still feel the after-effects of last night's drugs. I felt hideous.

I knew it showed on my face what I'd been up to. The dried sweat glistened with the chemicals I had consumed: acid, speed, ecstasy, and marijuana. I felt fragile as I walked, imagining that I would shatter if someone accidentally brushed past me.

As I tried to find my way home, I was positive that all the strangers on the street were talking about me, discussing how far I'd fallen, saying that I had come from such a good family, so *how could this have happened?*

I started to run. Without looking, I just ran to get home and out of sight. I knew if I was out any longer, or if any more people saw me like this, I was going to crack up and go totally insane, just like Evelyn. I'd be the next one to be locked up in that hideous mental patient ward. I ran as fast as I could. The illegal chemicals were the only thing keeping my feet moving, as I ran in my Doc Martin boots and sweaty clothes. I ran without even feeling tired. I stopped to catch my breath and hailed a taxi.

As the taxi driver drove me home, we passed The Wall. Through the taxi window, I saw three teenage boys, my age, working The Wall. They were just standing there, hanging around, doing nothing, just waiting to be picked up, to be used. They looked like westies. They came from the wrong side of town. I could tell just by looking at them that these boys hadn't grown up in the Eastern suburbs. I could also tell just by looking at them that they were the same as me: coming down. Only for them, it was from heroin, rather than ecstasy.

And it hit me. If I didn't come from a relatively well-to-do middle-class family, I could have ended up at The Wall by now. Perhaps I'd even be prostituting myself for drug money, pretending that I didn't mind having sex with men when I was out-of-it.

How else did those kids get there? Maybe they were just too out-of-it to go home. Were they on an all-night bender that they just didn't know how to end because the drugs were just so good? Were they high all the time? You'd have to be, to do what they were doing. The big difference between the boys working The Wall and me was that I had parents who hadn't thrown me out of their home, even though I'd given them plenty of reason to do so over the last year. Or, was it that my home wasn't so bad that I had to run away and never come back?

That Saturday night, for the first time in a very long time, I stayed home. I watched *Hey, Hey, It's Saturday* with Daryl Somers and Ossie Ostrich. It was so unbelievably lame. I remembered loving this show when I was younger, when it had been a morning show. I'd used to think it was the funniest show on TV. Now I felt so sad watching it I burst into tears. I imagined Tiffany getting ready to go out with the crew to have the best time of their lives. *Again.*

Sunday morning, I watched Video Hits, which got interrupted when the phone rang.

"Where did you disappear to?" It was Tiffany. Her voice was croaky.

"I had to leave." I didn't even bother to lie.

"Thanks for saying goodbye!" She sounded angry. "Can't believe you left me there with those guys. You know how crazy they are!"

"I didn't think anyone would miss me."

"I wish I had gone with you."

"Really?"

"Did you know that Eddie had been up for six days straight?"

"No. I'm not surprised, but..."

"Eddie had taken so much stuff last week that it was impossible for him to sleep. He injected himself with heroin to help him come down. He did it in front of me! It was so gross!"

I didn't know what to say.

She said, "I'm all for having a good time but I don't want to be around anyone who does the *hard stuff.*"

And it hit me, didn't Tiffany realise that somewhere we had crossed a line. Didn't she think we were doing hard stuff? Calling them party drugs just made them sound cute. But we were risking our health every time we went out for a dance.

I remembered the first night Tiffany and I had met Eddie. We'd been so impressed when he'd told us he'd taken ten ecstasy tablets in a single night. I'd thought Eddie had been joking or exaggerating. But he was for real. He was a full-on, hard-core clubber. He got so out-of-it that he was on the brink of killing himself.

COLD TURKEY

ON MONDAY MORNING, I put on my school uniform for the first week of term three while suffering from the worst comedown ever. It lasted for weeks. I went to class, but I was barely there. It was like being under water, watching my school friends and teachers talk while none of it made any sense. I turned up, sat with my friends, and tried to concentrate. I had so much homework to catch up on. There were economic theories to learn, math's problems to solve, and three novels to read for English class. It took every weekend of the term for me to catch up. Anna lent me some of her notes, which helped heaps.

Each weekend, I declined Tiffany's invitations to go out.

"God, Nathan it's like you've totally gone cold turkey."

It surprised me that I didn't give in. I forced myself to stay at home. I was panicking about how much homework and preparation I needed to do to get ready for the end-of-year qualifying exams for next year's HSC. There was no way I could handle repeating year 11. So, I crammed like a madman.

As The Group retreated from the Hordern dance parties, many other kids from Dover were discovering it, from the surfy crowd to the stoners, and even some of the nerdier kids. They started talking about their drug experiences and how they were going to dance parties. They were calling them raves by 1990. Everyone was going stompin'. It was like they were expecting us to be excited for them. From the way they spoke it was like they were trying to impress us or make us jealous that they were now a part of the scene. They were acting like they knew what it was all about just as we had several months ago.

"It's weird to see them just starting to get into it," Anna said. "I sort of feel sorry for them, getting into it right before the final year of their HSC."

"I know," I agreed. "They're acting just like we used to."

"You know, in six months' time, they're going to be going off the rails."

There was even a minor scandal when some kids from school took the Japanese exchange student to the Hordern, and he got hospitalised. He left in an ambulance, speaking half Japanese and half English. God knows what he'd taken. It was a cultural exchange that had gone terribly wrong.

For a long time, I believed that I was one of the few kids my age cool enough to take drugs and hang out on the scene. Now that so many other kids from school had started doing it, it made me realise that any dickhead can take drugs and think they're cool. What happened to me was that I'd gotten to a point where I could no longer have fun, even when I was on drugs. It was like I had no serotonin left in my brain to make me happy.

I just took drugs because that's the way the scene worked. I took drugs expecting them to automatically make life fun. Somewhere along the way, I forgot that only I could make that happen for myself. When I'd started to rely on something else to do it for me, that was when the problems had begun.

DANCE PARTY DISCIPLES

1990

ANNA TOLD ME about how she'd started going to the Hare Krishna temple in Darlinghurst on the weekends with her Mum. "They have a Sunday afternoon feast. You should come! It's so funny because I can see people we used to see at the dance parties, coming down as they listen to the teachings of Krishna consciousness while they wait for the free vegetarian food."

After several weeks of insisting we join her at the temple, Lee, Simon, Sarah, and I met Anna for the Sunday afternoon feast at the Hare Krishna temple on Darlinghurst Road. It was just near the Coca-Cola sign in Kings Cross.

I couldn't believe it when we saw Anna's mum, Eva, dressed in a bright orange and gold Indian sari. She was so nice to me, considering the last conversation we'd had was when her daughter had come home acting crazy after being supposedly spiked with LSD.

We listened to the Hare Krishna teachings and smirked as we danced along with the devotees chanting, "Hare Krishna, Hare Krishna, Hare Rama, Hare Rama."

Eva served food after we were lectured on how the material world was all about suffering and misery. The swami said, "The only way to find salvation is by surrendering ourselves back to Godhead, Lord Krishna, through chanting his divine name and giving up eating meat, taking drugs, and indulging in unfulfilling sexual acts."

I'd tuned out by this stage.

"Your mum's so cool and alternative," Lee complimented Anna.

"I know. I'm lucky. There aren't too many mothers who could guide their daughter through a bad acid trip!"

When I'd told my parents where I'd planned to spend my afternoon they had been horrified.

"Why are you hanging out with those *crazy orange cult people?*" Dad had protested. He was more worried about me spending one Sunday afternoon at the Hare Krishna temple than he'd ever been about me spending a Saturday night at the Hordern Pavilion.

Little did any of our parents know, but dance parties were like a cult. From the way they made us act, what we had to do to be a part of the scene, it was like a secret society where drugs, dancing, and the DJ became our god. We worshipped regularly and demonised anyone who didn't understand our movement. That's how we rolled when we were dance party disciples.

Time passed by slowly when I reached year 12. It was the very last year I had to spend at Dover Heights High. I couldn't wait to leave. The thought of not having to go to this school ever again made me ecstatic!

Turning eighteen was an incredible non-event. It wasn't like there was anything we hadn't tried in terms of booze and harder substances. Our relentless dancing and pill popping was replaced with relentless homework and studying.

When I turned eighteen, the first thing I did was to phone Campbell. But he was no longer living at the last phone number I had for him in Canberra. His mum's number had been disconnected so there was no way I could find him unless he called me, which he never did, and I never heard from Campbell again.

During year 12, I heard less and less from Tiffany. The last time we spoke, I wasn't even glad to hear from her. All Tiffany could talk about was what she'd taken, how cool it was, and what drugs she was going to take next. I realised how much I had changed and how much Tiffany had stayed the same. Even though we shared a laugh, the bond between us had disappeared. I was no longer impressed by the materialism, as the Hare Krishna sect would describe it, of Tiffany's going out stories.

To get through the HSC, I had to ignore clubbing and the dance party scene. It was dead and buried in my mind, so I could give myself a future that didn't involve getting wasted.

For Tiffany the scene was all there was. She lived for it completely and was never going to outgrow it. Tiffany was totally addicted. She was like a cult member from the party-people-sect. She couldn't complete a sentence without making a reference to drugs, clubs or the scene. When she spoke, she usually included all three items within the one sentence.

I am glad I experimented. Fortunately, I got to do so without the tragic consequence some face: *death*. Our group was extremely lucky by comparison to what happened to some we danced with. Most importantly, I was glad I'd had the will power to stop and walk out of the drug den in Darlinghurst. Because some people, like Tiffany, never stop and never get to walk away. It becomes a lifestyle.

To realise this, all I'd needed to do was to look around when I was on the dance floor. All around me there had been really, *really*, old people, like in their thirties and forties, who had still been partying like they were teenagers. Like Steven-the-Eckie-Man. He was so disconnected from reality that he had no idea how tragic he looked, grooving to the music and wearing clothes that were twenty years too young for him.

One day, Tiffany will probably be just like him. I can imagine her still on the dance floor when she reaches middle age, hallucinating on a handful of drugs, thinking she's still the coolest person there while a group of fourteen-year-olds, who've snuck into the party on fake IDs, point and laugh at the tragic old freak. Tiffany will be avoided by a whole new generation of club kids taking whatever substance will be in vogue to escape the drudgery of the high school experience and the awkwardness of their teenage years.

As for Michael and Sally, I bumped into Sally one day at the local library and she told me that they'd split up. Like me, she'd also stopped taking drugs. She'd had a massive wake-up call when Michael had began to deal at the Hordern. An undercover cop had eventually caught him. His parents had had to bail him out and he'd never made it through year 12. He'd dropped out before sitting the HSC.

Leading up to the HSC, I stayed up till midnight each day, reading and re-reading my notes. I committed them to what was left of my memory and my burned-out brain cells. Luckily, there were enough left to get me through.

FACE YOURSELF

WAITED AT MY parents' home the morning the postman was due to deliver the HSC results. The post was delivered at 10:30 a.m. When it came, I held my breath as I opened the mail.

The comments on my school report cards had been correct. I probably hadn't reached my full potential. I probably could have done much better if I'd focused on my studies instead of dance parties. But as it turned out, I still did much better than I'd expected and got a mark that put me in the top 20% of the state. It was no hallucination.

"I guess I'm going to university," I told Mum and Dad with pride.

"Good!" Mum smiled, "As long as you're happy."

I don't think they could believe I passed, considering.

In the mail, I also received another unexpected item. It was a envelope from Evelyn. The truth was that none of our group had visited Evelyn, as we'd said we would, or should have. We'd had too much homework and the idea was too depressing. Unfortunately, Evelyn didn't get better.

Eventually, Evelyn's Dad moved her back to New Zealand to live with her aunties and we hadn't heard from her since. I was sort of surprised because Evelyn had not written or called since the last time we'd seen her at the mental hospital in Darlinghurst.

Inside the envelope from Evelyn was a stack of yellow Post-it notes.

Evelyn had written a letter on practically a whole pad. *Guess she's still not well,* I thought with sadness and began to read the Post-it notes.

But by the time I finished reading it, somehow it meant more to me than my HSC score. What Evelyn had written was more like a story about our lives than a letter. Each yellow square brought back memories from when we were kids. The good times we'd shared before things had changed. It reminded me of the fun we'd had together before Evelyn had been institutionalised.

Even though Evelyn had asked me not to show the letter to anyone else, I had to show Anna, Lee, Simon, and Sarah because they were my best friends and I hoped they always would be. I let them read Evelyn's Post-it notes. It was something I had to share with my friends while they were still around. I hoped that they would understand.

"11:59 p.m., Saturday 13th, December 1990.

Dearest Nathan, I'm sitting on the floor of my bedroom, against my bed, comforted by a pillow. I'm listening to — just had to change the tape over, the side I was listening to ended. I'm listening to Bob Marley and burning incense — sandalwood. I have got four vegemite and butter sandwiches and all my photos in shoeboxes.

How is this for a soliloquy? Is that how you spell it? Who cares? Photos I'm looking at, a picture of the group in front of the pirate ship ride at the Royal Easter show in 1988 — it's all blurred. Worse than the photos Lee used to take of us. Next, a photo of you, Lee, Anna and I was getting ready to go to the Fun Love party in 1989. I don't think any of these photos are in order. Some family photos, one of my mum and one of my cat. I'm not telling you about all the photos because it would take all night.

Next envelope. This is a good lot. Mum and friend when she was 17, photo of me, Lee and Anna sleeping over at your place. You, Anna, Lee, and me under the shower on Bondi promenade in our bathers. Remember you drew a good pencil drawing of this photo? Next, you piggy backing me in Centennial Park (great shot!) Now a suggestive pose-mode shot of me, you, and Lee at my place before we went to Sweatbox Meltdown for my birthday.

You know I really miss you very much.

I have had this rehearsed for ages, just waiting for you to ask me why I just stopped talking to you guys and stopped hanging out with you. But you never asked, and no one ever visited me much so I never got the chance to tell you. Anyhow, now I can't remember what I really wanted to say, so this will only be a first draft.

I felt like you guys didn't like me anymore, so I cut contact. I got scared. Then we moved to Blacktown, and it was impossible to stay in touch. But before that happened, I had become so insecure and afraid because of the falseness of the group and the false feelings and actions. Going out, you guys took so many drugs, and I was losing myself to something I didn't like. But things are better now. I know who I am, and I know who loves me and who doesn't. I know who I love. I love Sarah, Anna, Elizabeth, Lee, Simon, and you. That must seem very silly since I distanced myself. Anyway, even though I can't show it to you anymore, I show it to the people in my memories very often.

I changed the tape. I got pins and needles in my foot. Back to the photos. Me at 13, Dad making funny faces, and me with someone I don't remember now.

When I finish this letter, I'm going to ask my auntie to mail it because I don't want to read it in the morning and not mail it. I don't want to just put it away for my own thoughts. I might as well take advantage of my drugged, happy mind. The doctors have got me on medication to stop the delusions. I'm feeling clear headed. That's why I decided to finally write to you.

I hope this makes sense. I hope you won't tell anyone I wrote to you because it is private. It means a lot to me, and I don't want anyone to discuss it or laugh at me because of it. Do you promise you won't tell and keep it to yourself?

I don't like gossip or being gossip. Sometimes, I feel good keeping a secret and knowing that even if you could tell, you wouldn't.

I wanted things to be different, but everybody picks their own life and their own friends and if you're not on their list, then it's their loss. I don't want to stop writing but my eyes are closing. I want to finish what I want to say. I felt the friendship we had was the best we could possibly offer each other at the time. I'm very happy we were close, and I was able to see the real Nathan, the warm side. I think you should show more of it and less of the exterior cool image that everyone else sees. I'll forever miss you and love you very much always.

Love Evelyn

PS - Please remember me and think happy thoughts that will make you happy too. I hope you like my story. Please face yourself, Nathan. I know you're gay. My brother saw you coming out of The Exchange Hotel late one night with another man. Shane told me all about it, but I made him swear he wouldn't tell anyone because I was afraid of what they'd do to you.

It's funny because I think we all sort of knew you were gay, but it didn't matter. We all loved you for who you were.

I'll be thinking of you ever more.

EPILOGUE

A FEW MONTHS LATER, the multicultural TV station SBS aired a documentary on ecstasy. It was about the rising phenomenon of dance parties in Australia and the effect it was having on Aussie youth.

I was a bit uncomfortable watching it because Mum and Dad were also keen to see it. The program talked about the unknowns, the dangers of the designer drug, how people overheat, how it can lead to long-term depression, psychosis, and even suicide.

When the program cut to real footage of a dance party, I couldn't contain my excitement once I recognised where it had been filmed. I knew the people who were dancing off-their-faces in the Hordern Pavilion. Without thinking how it would look to my parents, I pointed at the TV. "I know them!" I even recognised where this footage had been taken; it was from the Sweatbox, Let Them Eat Cake dance party.

Then there I was, dancing on the TV screen with Tiffany, Anna, Lee, Simon, and Sarah, all off our faces on ecstasy.

My parents couldn't believe what they were seeing. I was dancing wildly on a TV documentary about deadly designer drugs and the rising dance party culture ruining innocent young lives.

"You better not be taking any of that ecstasy!" Mum warned.

What was the point in telling them now?

"Sure, you would!" I rolled my eyes.

www.ingramcontent.com/pod-product-compliance
Lightning Source LLC
Chambersburg PA
CBHW070032260626
47159CB00005B/2019